MaryJanice Davidson has written in a variety of genres, including contemporary romance, paranormal romance, erotica, and non-fiction. She lives in Minnesota. Visit her website at www.maryjanicedavidson.net.

Also by MaryJanice Davidson

Undead and Unreturnable

MaryJanice Davidson

PIATKUS

PIATKUS

First published in Great Britain in 2006 by Piatkus Books
This paperback edition published in 2006 by Piatkus Books
First published in the US in 2005 by The Berkley Publishing Group,
a division of the Penguin Group (USA) Inc.

Copyright © 2005 by MaryJanice Davidson Alongi

Reprinted 2006 (twice), 2007, 2008

The moral right of the author has been asserted.

A CIP catalogue record for this book
is available from the British Library

ISBN 978-0-7499-3643-3

Typeset in Times by Palimpsest Book Production Limited,
Polmont, Stirlingshire
Printed and bound in Great Britain by Clays Ltd, St Ives plc

Piatkus Books
An imprint of
Little, Brown Book Group
100 Victoria Embankment
London EC4Y 0DY

An Hachette Livre UK Company
www.hachettelivre.co.uk

www.piatkus.co.uk

In honor of my grandfather,
John Opitz,
who taught me to do the best I could without complaint.
Which, like all important life lessons,
is lost on me.

ACKNOWLEDGMENTS

First and forever I must, must, must thank my children, who are brilliant, charming, and deft at entertaining themselves when Mom's locked in the office on deadline. They'd probably prefer my company to a few lines in a book, but as always, their expectations are too high; I'm just not that good a parent.

Another thousand thank-yous (to go with the kisses!) to my husband, Anthony, who came up with "sinister metrosexuality" and likes Betsy almost as much as he likes me. He puts up with the mood swings, speechifying, and ear-cutting that is part and parcel of living with a mass-market paperback author, and I adore him for it.

Thanks also to my PR person/best friend/evil side-kick Jessica Growette, who I swear lies awake at night thinking about how to get my name out there. Which is cool, if creepy.

The Magic Widows, of course, must also be thanked. I learn something every Tuesday. Even better, sometimes I retain it!

Special thanks to Carl Hiaasen, John Sandford, and Laurell K. Hamilton for continually showing me how it's done.

Finally, thank you to the readers who enjoy reading about Betsy's comings and goings and who wanted to know where she went next. Thanks for hopping in and coming for the ride.

AUTHOR'S NOTE

After seeing all the books, movies, magazines, and National Enquirer articles out there about serial killers, I got a little curious. After some research, I found that the actual number of estimated psycho killer nutjobs running around is anywhere between ten and five hundred. (For obvious reasons, it's tough to come up with an exact number.)

Let's say the experts are way off, and triple the guesstimate: one thousand, five hundred. There are about three hundred million people in the United States. So roughly .0000005 percent of the population is made up of serial killers. Needless to say, chances are you're not going to trip over one in your driveway.

Betsy, of course, has problems most of us will never, ever have to deal with. She and Detective Nick Berry win the serial killer lottery in this tale, but, like drinking blood and endless police paperwork, it's not something most of the rest of the population has to worry about.

Also, colic is bad. But it doesn't last forever.

From the Book of the Dead:

"And the Queene shall noe the dead, all the dead, and neither shall they hide from her nor keep secrets from her."

And:

"And she will noe Evil in many forms, and defeat it should that be her will, and be the Protector and Avenger of all the dead, for as long as shalt be the will of the Queene."

"Just like a spider with a line of silk! Did you ever see them throw themselves out into space to weave? They're taking a chance, every single time. They got to do it or else they'd never create anything. But I bet it don't feel good, even to a spider."

—OLIVIA GOLDSMITH,
Fashionably Late

"It's not a bad little tree, really. It just needs a little love."

—LINUS,
A Charlie Brown Christmas

"There's more of gravy than of grave about you, whatever you are!"

—CHARLES DICKENS,
A Christmas Carol

Undead and Unreturnable

PROLOGUE

From the St. Paul Pioneer Press
December 15, 2005

THIRD WOMAN FOUND SLAIN. Minneapolis, Minnesota.

The body of an Edina resident was found this morning at approximately six-thirty A.M. Cathie Robinson, 26, was found in the parking lot of the Lake Street Wal-Mart. Forensics show that she had been strangled. She had been reported missing on December 13. She is believed to be the third victim of the so-called Driveway Killer, who has so far claimed at least three local victims.

Detective Nick Berry, who has been working with the FBI since the second victim, Martha Lundquist, was found on November 23, said the investigation is pursuing several leads. "This is our top priority," Berry said. "Nothing else even comes close."

Ms. Lundquist was reported missing on November 8, and her body was found in the parking lot of a White Bear Lake Target store on November 10.

The FBI has profiled the killer, who appears to be choosing tall blond women with light-colored eyes and short hair. Although an arrest is "imminent," Berry warns Minneapolis women to use caution when leaving their places of business.

It is believed that the Driveway Killer has also struck in Iowa, Missouri, and Arkansas.

The FBI and local police believe that the first local victim was Katie Johnson, 27, who was reported missing on October 28 and whose body was found on November 4 in the parking lot of the Lakeville McStop.

From the Star Tribune
December 17, 2005

BORN, to Antonia Taylor and John Peter Taylor
of Edina, Minnesota, a boy, Jonathon Peter Taylor
II, at 12:05 A.M. on December 15 at Fairview
Ridges Edina.

CHAPTER 1

This is how my tombstone read:

ELIZABETH ANNE TAYLOR
APRIL 25, 1974–APRIL 25, 2004
OUR SWEETHEART, ONLY RESTING

"That's just so depressing," my best friend, Jessica Watkins, observed.

"It's weird." My sister, Laura Goodman, was staring. "That is very, very weird."

"Our sweetheart, only resting?" I asked. "What the hell's that supposed to mean?"

"I think it's nice," my sister said, a little hesitantly. She looked like a dirty old man's dream with her long, butterscotch-blond hair, big blue eyes, and red peacoat. You know how ministers' kids will sometimes go wild when they finally get away from their parents? Laura was the devil's daughter (no, really), so her way of rebelling was to be as nice and sweet as possible. A dastardly plan. "It's a little different. Most of the people I know would have gone with a Bible verse, but your mama certainly didn't have to."

"Given how things turned out," Jess replied, running a hand over her skinned-back black hair, "it's a little prophetic, don't you think?" As usual, when she put her hair up, she pulled it back so tightly, the arch of her eyebrows made her look constantly amazed. Though it's possible, given where we were standing, that she really *was* amazed.

"I think standing in front of my own grave is the last place I want to be on the seventeenth day of December, is what I think." Depressing *and* creepy. Must be the holidays.

Jessica sighed again and rested her forehead on my shoulder. "Poor Betsy. I can't get over it. You were so young!"

Laura smirked a little. "Like turning thirty wasn't enough of a trauma. Poor Betsy."

"So young!"

"Will you pull yourself together, please? I'm right here." I stuck my hands into my coat pockets and sulked. "What is it, like ten below out? I'm freezing."

"You're always freezing. Don't bitch if you're going to go outside without your gloves. And it's thirty-five degrees, you big baby."

"Would you like my coat?" Laura said. "I don't really feel the cold."

"Another one of your sinister powers," Jessica said. "We'll add it to the list with weapons made of hellfire and always being able to calculate a 22 percent tip. Now Bets, run this by me again . . . how'd your tombstone finally show up here?"

I explained, hopefully for the last time. I had, of course, died in the spring. Rose in the early dawn hours the day of my funeral and gone on undead walkabout. Because my body was MIA, the funeral was cancelled.

But my mother, who had been in a huge fight with my dad and stepmom about what to spend on my marble tombstone, had rushed to order the thing. By the time it was finished, no funeral, no service, no burial. (My family knew the truth about what I was now, and so did Jessica. My other coworkers and friends had been told the funeral had been a joke, one in very poor taste.)

So anyway, my tombstone had been in storage the last six months. (My stepmother had been pushing for plain, cheap granite, with my initials and my dates of death and birth; a penny saved is a penny earned, apparently. My dad, as he always did when my mom and Antonia were involved, stayed out of it.)

After a few months, the funeral home had politely contacted my mother and asked what she'd like to do with my tombstone. Mom had the plot and the stone paid for, so she had them stick it in the dirt the day before yesterday, and mentioned it at lunch yesterday. You know how it goes:

"Waiter, I'll have the tomato soup with Parmesan croutons, and by the way, honey, I had your tombstone set up in the cemetery yesterday."

Jessica and Laura had been morbidly curious to see it, and I'd tagged along. What the hell, it made for a break from wedding arrangements and Christmas cards.

"Your mom," Jessica commented, "is a model of scary efficiency."

Laura brightened. "Oh, Dr. Taylor is so nice."

"And just when I think your stepmother can't get any lamer . . . no offense, Laura." The Ant was technically Laura's birth mother. It was a long story.

"I'm not offended," she replied cheerfully.

"Have you two weirdos seen enough?"

"Wait, wait." Jessica plopped the bouquet of cream-colored calla lilies on my grave. I nearly shrieked. I'd sort of assumed she'd picked those up for one of the eighty thousand tables in our house. Not for my *grave*. Ugh! "There we go."

"Let's bow our heads," Laura suggested.

"No *way*. You're both fucking ill."

"Language," my sister replied mildly.

"We're not praying over my grave. I'm massively creeped out just being here. That would be the final, ultimately too-weird step, ya weirdo."

"*I'm* not the one on a liquid diet, O vampire queen. Fine, if you won't pray, then let's book."

"Yeah," I said, casting one more uneasy glance at my grave. "Let's."

CHAPTER 2

"Good evening, Your Majesty."

"Tina, baby," I called, dumping more cream in my tea. "Have a seat. Have a cup."

"How long have you been up?"

"Two hours or so," I said, trying not to sound smug. God had answered my prayers and lately I'd been waking up around four in the afternoon. Of course, I lived in Minnesota in December, so it was just as dark at four as it was at eight, but still.

"But you . . . you haven't seen the paper?" Tina sat down across from me, the *Trib* folded under her arm. She put it next to her and ignored the teapot. "Not yet?"

"I don't like the sound of *that*. Not one bit."

Tina hesitated, and I braced myself. Tina was an old vampire, ridiculously beautiful like most vampires, totally devoted to Sinclair and, to a lesser extent, me. She had made Sinclair, way back when, and helped us both win our crowns more recently, protected us, lived with us (not like that, ewww!) . . . she was like a major domo, except little and cute. So I guess she'd be a minor domo.

She had long, taffy-colored hair, which she usually piled up in an efficient knot, and enormous dark eyes. Big brownish-black anime eyes. Though she barely came up to my chin, she gave off an almost noble air. Like Scarlett O'Hara's mother Ellen, I'd never seen Tina's shoulders touch the back of any chair; I'd never seen her even slouch. She was also insanely smart and never forgot anything. She was a lot more queenlike than me, to tell the truth.

Anyway, my point was, she handled with aplomb the sort of situations that would drive most of us clinically insane or at least irritable. And she was hesitating. She was *nervous*.

Lord, help me be strong. "I guess you better tell me."

She silently unfolded the paper and handed it to me. Births and deaths. I read the announcement. "Huh," I said with total unsurprise. "My brother was born days ago, and they didn't bother to tell me. How about that."

Tina was actually cringing in her chair and opened her eyes wide at my remarks. "That's . . . that's all? That's your only comment?"

"Oh, come on. I grew up with those people. This isn't exactly atypical behavior. I guess I better get over to the house and pay my respects. Let's see . . . we're supposed to meet with the florist tonight, but I seriously doubt Sinclair's gonna mind if I reschedule that . . . and Jess and I are supposed to have a late supper, but she won't want me to miss this . . . yeah, I'll go see the baby tonight."

Tina's perfect, smooth forehead was wrinkled in surprise. "I must say, Majesty, you're taking this much better than I anticipated."

"I was sort of expecting it. I've been keeping half an eye on the birth announcements . . . just haven't had a chance to get to them today. The baby's early . . . I didn't think the Ant was due until January."

"She might have gotten her dates mixed up," Tina suggested. "It's possible she miscalculated the date of her last menstrual—"

"I'm trying to kill my unholy thirst, here," I reminded her.

"Sorry."

I took another look at the paper. "So brother Jon. You know, the last baby the Ant had was the daughter of the devil. Wonder what you're gonna be like?"

CHAPTER 3

"Your father's not here," the Ant said. Although she looked haggard, her pineapple-colored hair helmet was in perfect shape. She was clutching a baby monitor in her unpolished fingers, and a steady, monotonous crying was coming out of it. "He's not back until tomorrow."

"I'm here to see the baby, Antonia. You know, my brother? Congratulations, by the way."

She was still hanging in the doorway, keeping me standing on the front step. "It's not a good time, Betsy."

"It never is. Really, for either of us. You look terrible," I said cheerfully.

She glared. "I'm busy now, so you'll have to come back."

"Look, Antonia, how do you want to do this? I can keep

calling and keep coming by and you can keep blowing me off, and I can bitch to my father who will eventually get tired of being in the middle and make you let me see the baby, or you can let me in tonight and get it over with."

She swung the door open wide. "Fine, come in."

"Thank you so much. You're too kind. So have you gained a ton of weight lately?" I asked, shrugging out of my coat. Then I remembered that I was constantly cold and wouldn't be staying long and put it back on. "Not that you don't look, you know, good."

"I have to check on Jon," she said, scowling at the monitor. "The doctor says it's colic. Your father left me with him."

"Yeah, that's kind of his thing."

"We named him after your father," she added proudly, if inanely.

"But Dad's name is John. With an H. The baby's name is Jon, which, as I'm sure you know, being his mother, is short for Jonathon, which is spelled totally differently." My lips were moving; could she understand me? Maybe it was time to get out the Crayolas.

She glared. "Close enough. He's Jon Peter, just like your father."

I gave up. "Which bedroom have you set up as a nursery?"

She pointed to the south end of the hallway at the top of the stairs . . . the bedroom farthest from the master bedroom. Surprise. I mounted the stairs, and she was right behind me.

"You'd better not bite him," she snarked, which I didn't dignify with an answer. The Ant felt (and said, loudly, all the time) it was really thoughtless of me to not stay dead, and felt my fellow vampires were a bad element. That last one was a tough case to argue against. "You just better not. In fact, maybe you shouldn't touch him at all."

"I promise, I don't have a cold." I opened the door—I could hear the baby yowling through the wood—and walked into the nursery, which was overdone in Walt Disney Pooh. "Ick, at least do the original Pooh."

"We're redoing it next week," she replied absently, staring into the crib. "All my Little Mermaid stuff showed up from eBay."

Yikes, no wonder he was screaming. I looked down at him and saw nothing special: a typical red-faced newborn with a shock of black hair, little eyes squeezed into slits, mouth open in the sustained *"EeeeeeYAH eeeeeeYAH eeeeeeYAH"* of a pissed-off young baby.

He was dressed in one of those little sack things, like Swee'Pea, a pale green that made the poor kid look positively yellow. His little limbs didn't have much fat on them; they were sticklike. His teeny fists were the size of walnuts.

Poor kid. Stuck in this overly big house with a Walt Disney theme, the Ant as his mom, and green swaddling clothes. It was too much to ask of anybody, never mind someone who hadn't been on the planet for even a week. If I could have wept for him, I would have.

"Here," the Ant said, and handed me a small bottle of Purell.

I rolled my eyes. "I'm not contagious."

"You're dead. Ish."

I debated arguing but then just gave up and gave my hands a quick wash. Baby Jon wailed the entire time. I felt a little like wailing myself as I handed the bottle back.

I didn't ask if I could pick him up; I just did it, carefully supporting his head. (I remembered that much from my baby-sitting days.) He finished up a final *"EeeeeeYAH!"* and then just laid there, gasping.

"I don't want you to—" the Ant began and then cut herself off and stared at her son. "My God, that's the first time he's stopped crying in hours."

"I guess he likes me."

"Give him back."

I handed Baby Jon over, and as soon as he was out of my arms he started howling again. The Ant hastily handed him back to me, and he quit.

I grinned—I couldn't help it. A new vampire power! Newborns did my unholy bidding. Even better, the Ant was looking as green as Baby Jon's outfit.

"Well," I said loudly, because I'd handed him back again and I had to be heard over the shrieking, "I'll be going now."

"Wait!"

Heh.

CHAPTER 4

I popped open the kitchen door and practically leaped into the middle of the floor. "I have returned!" I cried.

"Yeah, so have I," Jessica said. She was still in her caramel-colored coat, a man's coat that came almost to her ankles, and had her knitting bag in one hand and her gloves in the other. Nobody else looked up. Maybe I'd better rethink the dramatic entrance; too many people were used to it. "Thanks for canceling on me, you evil whore."

"Oh, come on, like you really cared that I went over there and bugged the shit out of the Ant. And I have to cancel on you tomorrow, too, because I'm"—I paused for dramatic impact—"baby-sitting my baby brother."

Jessica gaped. "You're doing what to the baby?"

Tina and Sinclair actually looked up. "We didn't catch that one, dear," Sinclair told me.

"You all caught it. You heard exactly what I said." I pulled my cold hands out of my pockets and blew on them, which did zero good. "Yeah, that's right. I'm baby-sitting. The baby likes me, and even though the Ant doesn't, she's desperate to get out of the house. So I'm going back tomorrow night."

"Back . . . into your stepmother's home."

"To be alone with her baby," Tina clarified.

"Your stepmother's baby," Sinclair added.

"I know! It's a Christmas miracle!"

"Well, I'll come with," Jessica decided. "Keep you company. And I'd like to see—John, is it?"

"Jon. Yeah. It'll be fun! Weird. But fun. We can zap some popcorn and 'forget' it in the back of her closet." I tossed my keys on the counter and crossed the room. "What are you guys working on?"

Eric Sinclair leaned back so I could take a look. He was the king of the vampires, my lover, my fiancé, my nemesis, and my roommate. It had been, to put it mildly, an interesting year.

As usual, I was so distracted by Sinclair's essential deliciousness, I almost forgot to look at the book they were so engrossed in. He was just so . . . well, yummy. Yummy and great-looking and tall and broad-shouldered and so so fine. Should-be-against-the-law fine. Big hands. Big smile. Big teeth. Big everything. Oofta. After months of fighting my attraction to him, I didn't have to anymore, and baby, I was gorging. We both were. It was nice not to be looking at him out of the corner of my eye all the time. We were getting married. We were in love. We were supposed to be drooling all over each other.

I brushed some of his dark hair off his forehead, tried not to stare longingly into his black eyes, let my hand wander down to his lapel, and finally tore my gaze back to the table. In half a second, my good mood evaporated like the Ant's taste at a sample sale.

"What the *hell* is *that* doing here?"

"Darling, your grip—" He put his hand on my wrist and gently disengaged me, because I'd twisted the cloth of his lapel in my fist and, knowing him, he was less worried about the damage to his windpipe than ruining the line of his clothing.

"Don't get upset," Tina began.

"Ahhh! Ahhh!" I ahhh'd, pointing.

"The UPS man brought it," she continued.

Jessica and I stared at her.

"No, really," she said.

"The UPS guy brought *that*?" Jessica squeaked, also pointing at the Book of the Dead.

"And a box from your mother," Tina added helpfully.

"Christ, I'd hate to see what's in the other box!"

"I thought we—" Jessica glanced at Sinclair, who was as smooth-faced as ever, though his black eyes were gleaming in a way that made the hair on my arms want to leave. "I thought it was gone for good."

"Shit, shit, shit," I muttered. It was open—open!—and I slammed it closed. "Shit! Don't look at it. Shit! Why were you looking at it?"

"Oh, well, the best-laid plans and all of that." Sinclair smiled, but he didn't look especially happy. "Better luck next time, and by that I mean, don't you *dare* try it again."

Long story short: I'd read the Book of the Dead around Halloween and had gone nuts for a while. Really nuts. Biting and hurting my friends nuts. Even now, three months later, I was still so desperately ashamed of how I'd acted, I could hardly think about it. I had punished myself by wearing Kmart sneakers for a month, but even that didn't seem to strike the right note of penitence.

The up side was, now I could rise from my deep, dark slumber in the late afternoon, instead of being conked from dawn to dusk. But it wasn't enough of a trade-off for me, and I'd thrown the Book into the Mississippi River, and good riddance.

Sinclair had been coldly furious, and Tina hadn't been especially happy with me, either. Historical document, priceless beyond rubies, invaluable soothsaying tool, blah-blah. He hadn't shut me out of his bed, but the entire time we were having sex that night, he never stopped with the lecturing. And in his head (I can read his mind, though he doesn't know that—yet), he was pissed. It had been a new kind of awful. But at the time, I thought it was a small price to pay to be rid of it.

And now it was back.

"Shit," I said again, because for the life of me, I couldn't think of anything else.

"Well," Jessica said, staring at the Book, "I have some good news."

"This is a really good fake?"

"No. I've just finished my last crochet class. Now I can teach George another stitch."

"Oh." I managed to tear my gaze from the Book. "Well, that is good news. That's—really good."

"How was your grave?" Tina asked politely.

"Don't change the subject."

"But it's so tempting."

"What are we going to do with *that*?"

"Jessica already changed the subject. And I thought we'd put it back in the library."

"Where it belongs, and should never have been taken from in the first place," Sinclair added silkily.

"Hey, my house, my library, my book."

"Hardly," he snitted.

"Besides, it's *our* house," Jessica said, which was kind, because she paid the mortgage. Sinclair paid a pittance in rent, and I didn't pay anything. We'd used the proceeds from the sale of my old, termite-ridden place to put a partial down payment on the mansion.

"It's dangerous," I said, which was futile because I knew when I was beat.

"It's a tool. Like any tool, it depends on how you use it." Sinclair started to get up. "I'll remove it to the library."

"Nuh-uh." I put my hand on his shoulder and pushed. It was like trying to budge a boulder. "C'mon, siddown already. I'll put it in the library. I promise not to pitch it into the river on the way."

After a long moment, he sat. I awkwardly scooped up the Book (it was about two feet long, a foot wide, and six inches thick) and shuddered; it was warm. The vampire bible, bound in human skin, written in blood, and full of prophecies that were never wrong. Trouble was, if you read the thing too long, it drove you nuts. Not "I'm having a bad day and feel bitchy" nuts, or PMS nuts. "I think I'll commit felony assault on my friends and rape my boyfriend" nuts.

"I'm going to the basement," Jessica said after the long silence. "I'm going to show George the new stitch."

"Wait," I grunted, hefting the Book.

"C'mon, I want to show him now, so he can practice."

"I said wait, dork. You're not supposed to be alone with him, remember?"

"He's never hurt me. He's never even looked in my direction. Not since you keep him full of your icky queen blood."

"Nevertheless," Sinclair said, free of the Book and now picking up the *Wall Street Journal,* "you are not to be alone with him, Jessica. Ever."

She scowled, but she was scowling at the paper, which was now in front of Sinclair's face. I almost laughed. Dismissed. He did it to me all the time.

"Let me dump this thing in the libe," I said, staggering toward the door—it was hard to carry something and not gag at the same time—"and I'll be right with you. Anything's better than this."

"That's a bold statement," Tina observed, stirring her coffee. "Especially since you've recently been to your stepmother's."

"Har," I said, and made my way toward the library.

CHAPTER 5

"Well!" I said brightly, descending the stairs. "That was about the most disgusting thing ever."

"And you drink blood every week."

"Ugh, don't remind me. George? Honey, you up?"

We went to the other end of the basement (the place was huge; it ran the length of the mansion and, among other things, we'd had decapitated bodies down there as well as a body butter party) and found George in his room, busily crocheting another endless yarn link. Sky blue, this time.

He looked up alertly when we walked into his room and then went back to his crocheting. The scary thing about George was how normal he was starting to look. He was tall and lean, with a swimmer's build, shoulder-length golden brown hair, and dark brown eyes. When he'd been more feral, it was tough to see the man under all the mud. Now that he was on a steady diet of my blood, it was hard to see the feral vampire under the man.

He was too thin, but he had the best butt I'd ever seen, never mind that my heart belonged to Sinclair (and his butt). His eyes were the color of wet mud, and occasionally a flash of his intelligence gleamed out at me. Or maybe that was just wishful thinking.

He seemed only to like me, which was fair, because I was the only one who hadn't wanted to stake him and his fellow Fiends. The others were at a mansion in Minnetonka, being cared for by another vampire. Unlike George, the other Fiends had no desire to do anything but crawl around on all fours and drink blood out of buckets.

I wasn't really sure what to do about the Fiends, thus my great and all-encompassing "live and let die" policy. The asshat who used to run the vampires was a big experiment fan—you know, like the Nazis. And one of his favorite things to do was starve newly risen vampires.

Thus, the Fiends: feral, inhuman, and not so great with the vocalizing. Or the walking. Or the—anyway. They were monsters, but it wasn't their fault . . . the *real* monster had gotten to them first.

All I could do was try to look out for them . . . and keep George amused. Unlike the others, George liked to drink my blood every couple days or so. Unlike the others, George was walking.

It was very strange.

"Check it out, baby," Jessica said, bringing out a crochet hook of her own and showing it to him. Then she glanced at me. "Uh, he's eaten this week, right?"

"Unfortunately, yes." I glared at my wrist, which had already healed over. I only liked sharing blood with Sinclair; the rest of it sort of squicked me out. And I only did it with Sinclair during, um, intimate moments.

Sad to say, my blood (queen blood, sigh) was the only thing making George better. Three months ago, he was covered with mud, naked, howling at the moon, and eating the occasional rapist. Yarn work in my basement and consenting to red Jockeys was a big damn improvement.

"Like this," Jessica was saying, showing him what looked, to me, like an incredibly complicated stitch. But then, I'd tossed out my counted cross-stitch patterns at age sixteen after declaring them way too hard. Crocheting and knitting . . . yurrgh.

My mom tried to teach me to knit once, and it went like this: "Okay, I'll do it really slowly so you can follow." Then the needles flashed and she'd knitted half a scarf. That's about when I gave up on all crafts.

"And then . . ." Jess was murmuring, "through the loop . . . like this."

He hummed and took the yarn from her.

"What's next on the wedding agenda?"

"Um . . ." I shut my eyes and thought. My Sidekick was upstairs, but I knew most of the wedding details by heart.

"Flowers. I'm still pushing for purple irises and yellow alstromeria lilies, and Sinclair is still pretending we're not getting married."

"What's the new date?"

"September 15."

Jessica frowned. "That's a Thursday."

I stared at her. "How do you know *that*?"

"Because it's the date my parents died, so I try to get out to the cemetery then. And I remember, last September was a Wednesday."

"Oh." We did not discuss Jessica's mother and father. Ever. "Well, what difference does it make? Like Sinclair cares? Like the other vampires do? Oh, what, we've all got to get up early for work the next morning?"

"How many times have you changed the date? Four?"

"Possibly," I said grudgingly. It had been, respectively, February 14 (I know, I know, and to give me credit, I *did* scrap the idea eventually), April 10, July 4, and now September 15.

"I don't understand why you don't just get it done, hon. You've wanted this how long? And Sinclair is agreeable and everything? I mean, what the hell?"

"There just hasn't been time to get all the details taken care of. I *have* been solving murders and dodging bloody coups," I bitched. "That's why I keep moving the date. There aren't enough hours in the day. Night."

Jessica didn't say anything. Thank God.

"Look!" I pointed. George was crocheting the new stitch she'd just showed him. "Wow, he's catching on."

"Next: the knit stitch."

"Can't you ever rest on your laurels? Let the guy make a blanket or something."

"And after that," she said confidentially, "we're going to start with reading and math."

"Oh, boy."

"He already knows how. He must. It's just a matter of reminding him."

"Yeah, that's what it's a matter of."

She ignored that. "So what else? Flowers? And then what? You've got the gown picked out."

"Yup. Picked it up last week. The nice thing about being dead is one fitting pretty much did the trick."

"Well, there you go. What else?"

"The tasting menu."

"How are you going to pull *that* off?"

"It's wine for them, juice and stuff for the rest of us." I heard myself say that and wondered: *Who did I think "us" was?*

"Oh. Good work. And?"

"The cake. Not for us." There was that word again! "But there will be some regular guys there. You, Marc, my folks."

"The Ant?"

"I'm inviting her."

"You are? Well, maybe she'll have a face-lift scheduled that day."

I perked up. "Maybe. You think? Anyway. I'm leaning toward chocolate with raspberry ganache filling, topped with chocolate-covered strawberries. And, you know, ivory basket-weave fondant icing."

"Stop, you're making me hungry."

"And I've been trying to get Sinclair to go tux shopping."

"Why? He's got a million of them."

"Yeah, but this is *the* tux. The mother of all tuxes. The wedding day tux. He needs something special."

"Maybe in a nice powder blue," she suggested.

I laughed. "Or canary yellow. Can you imagine? Wouldn't he just die?"

"Again. Actually, he seems pretty close to it. He, uh, doesn't seem all that interested in the details. I mean, more than most guys. Which is weird, given his cool metrosexualness."

I hadn't heard that exact term (which had been sooo trendy the year before but was now woefully overused) applied to Sinclair, but I only had to mull it over for half a second before I realized she was right. He had a big dick, adored women, didn't mind kicking the shit out of bad guys, insisted on redecorating all the parlors, was a foodie and a tea snob. Ah, the love of my life. Great in bed and would only drink tea from leaves, not bags. Whodathunkit.

I sat down on one of the chairs and watched George busily crochet. Speaking of metrosexuals. He'd already done four inches across.

"You know how it is. Sinclair's like a tick, he gets so stubborn. 'We're married by vampire law, a ceremony is redundant,' blah-blah."

"That's tough," she said sympathetically. She was digging

around in her craft bag and tossing more skeins of yarn to George. A wool rainbow flew through the air: red, blue, yellow, purple. "But you know it's not a question of love. You know that, right?"

"I guess . . ."

"Come on, Bets. You guys got that cleared up at Halloweentime. He worships you. He'd do anything for you. He's *done* anything for you. It's not his fault he's considered you guys to be married for the last eight months."

"Mmm. Did you know, our wedding is going to be the first vampire monarch wedding in the history of dead people?"

"Something for the diary. Vampire *monarch* wedding?"

"Umm. Because vampires get married now and again. And a vampire/human couple will get married—like Andrea and Daniel. But I guess since the Book of the Dead claims we're already married, it's never actually been done."

"So?"

"Exactly," I said firmly. "Exactly! Who gives a damn if it's never been done? No reason not to do it. But I'm not taking his name."

Jessica burst out laughing. "I just realized. If you did, you'd be Sink Lair."

"Don't even tell me."

"Better not tell *him*. He's kind of a traditionalist."

Exactly what had been worrying me lately.

CHAPTER 6

One of the ghosts came to bug me while I was updating my diary. I don't know why I bothered. I'd write full steam for about a week and then totally lose interest. My closet was full of ninety journals that were only used through the first fifteen pages.

Marc had just left after begging me, once again, to have a carrot cake instead of chocolate. The maniac. We exchanged cross words and then he huffed out. Jessica was asleep. (It was two A.M.) Tina was out on the town, probably feeding. (I was careful not to ask.) Sinclair was somewhere in the house.

And the ghost was standing in front of my closet with her back to me, bent forward like a butler bowing from the waist, her head stuck through the door. I don't even know why I turned around. She'd been as noisy as a dead battery. I just did. And there she was.

I sat there for a moment and took a steadying breath, ignoring the instant dizziness. This happened occasionally. Part of the queen thing. The first time I'd been scared shitless. Ironically, I was terrified of dead things.

I wasn't used to it, exactly, but at least these days I didn't go tearing out of the room to cringe in the driveway.

"Um," I said.

She pulled her head out and looked at me, amazed. "You have a *lot* of shoes."

"Thanks."

"More than Payless."

I concealed a shudder. "Thanks." We stared at each other. She was a small strawberry blonde, about five foot nothing, with her hair pulled up in an I-Dream-of-Jeannie ponytail. She was blue-eyed and had lots of caramel-colored freckles all over her face and hands. She was wearing beat-up blue jeans and a booger-colored turtleneck. Battered black flats; no socks. Freckles on the tops of her feet, too.

"I'm, ah, sorry to bother you. But I think I—I think I might be dead."

"I'm really sorry to have to tell you this," I replied, "but you are."

She sat down on my floor and cried for about ten minutes. I didn't know what to say or do. I couldn't leave, though that was my first impulse—to give her some privacy. But I was afraid she'd take it the wrong way.

I couldn't touch her—my hands went right through ghosts, and it was horrible. Like plunging your limbs into an ice bath. So a supportive pat or hug was out of the question. "There, there" seemed unbelievably lame. So did going back to my journal. So I just stayed in my desk chair and watched her and waited.

After a while, she said, "Sorry."

"You're totally entitled."

"I knew, you know. I just—hoped I was wrong. But nobody—you're the only one—nobody can see me. The EMTs couldn't see me, and the guys in the morgue, and my boyfriend."

"How did you know to come here?"

"I—I don't know."

"Okay." Dammit! If the ghosts knew, nobody was telling. I didn't know if there was a sign outside my house ("She sees dead people") that only the dead could see, or what. Not that it made much difference. But I was curious.

She sighed. "I was hoping you could do me a favor."

"Sure," I said at once. I knew from experience that it was just easier (and quicker) to give them what they wanted. Otherwise, they hung around and talked to me at the most awkward moments. Ever been interrupted by a ghost while you're washing your hair? Or going down on your fiancé? Awkward. "What can I do for you?"

"Well, the last thing I remember—the last time anybody else could see me—I had just run out of our apartment building. Mine and my boyfriend's. We had this big wicked fight because he thought I was cheating on him, but I swear I wasn't!"

"Okay."

"And if you could just—go see him? And tell him? I only had dinner with the guy twice. I wasn't going to do anything. It's Denny I love. I'm so mad I didn't realize that before running out in front of the—anyway. I hate the thought—I *hate* the thought—of Denny thinking to the end of his days that the last thing I did was cheat on him. I mean, I can't sleep for worrying about it." She paused. "Not that I could anyway. I think. But it's really bothering me. It—it really is."

"I'll be glad to go see him. I'll do it first thing tomorrow night."

"I live in Eagan," she said. Then she gave me excellent directions, which I wrote down in my journal.

"No problem at all. It's done."

"Thank you so m—" Then she looked extremely surprised and popped out of sight. This was also expected. It was like whenever they got whatever-it-was off their chests, they could go to . . . wherever.

Poor thing. I was getting all kinds. At least she didn't feel bad about stealing or a dead mom or criminal assault or something awful like that.

I went back to my journal and realized she'd never told me her name—and I'd never bothered to ask. This bothered me a lot . . . was I getting jaded? Well, obviously I was, but how bad?

Dammit.

CHAPTER 7

The next night, I pulled back into my driveway after going about my little errand. The boyfriend—Denny—had been tearfully receptive to my news. That was the weirdest part of all the ghost stuff . . . not only did the ghosts feel better after they told me what they wanted, but whomever I told also felt better. Believed me, unquestioningly. None of that Whoopi Goldberg skepticism in *Ghost*. No, it was always, "Thank you so much, thank God you told me, now I can get on with my life, are you sure you don't want any coffee?" Very strange. But better than the alternative, I figured.

There was a shiny red Dodge Ram pickup in the driveway, parked crookedly, one tire actually in the grass. I had no idea who the hell it was—no one I knew drove a red truck—and wondered if I wanted to go in.

See, things started out innocently enough—a visitor, a comment, finding out a new vampire rule—and the next thing I know, I'm up to my tits in undead politics, or attempted revolutions, or dead bodies.

It had gotten so that I distrusted everything new, no matter how minor. And that was a *big* truck. Not minor at all. With a super-cab, no less. It could have brought five new trouble-makers to my house, easy.

I looked at my watch. It was only six-thirty. But that meant Tina and Sinclair were up, at least. So if it was something annoying, I'd at least have help. Maybe I could fob the whole thing off on them.

Shit, maybe it didn't have a single thing to do with me!

Nah.

I let myself in the front door in time to hear a cracking adolescent male voice yell, "I'll go if Betsy wants me to go, so cram it, Sinclair!"

I knew that piping, wanting-to-be-deep-but-not-quite-making-it voice. Jon Delk, former head of the Blade Warriors, current pain in my ass. After the Warriors disbanded last summer, he'd gone back to the family farm. I hadn't heard from him since. What the hell could have brought him back? Nothing good, that's what.

"Tina," I heard Sinclair say casually, and because I knew that voice, I started running, "see our little friend out."

"Go ahead, vampire. You just lay one dead finger on me."

"Okay," Tina said cheerfully and then I burst into the kitchen.

"Stop it! Whatever it is, play nice, you bums."

"Betsy." His face—his young, wholesome, ridiculously handsome face—brightened when he saw me, and he smiled so wide his dimples showed. "Hey. Great to see you. You look great. It's really . . . uh . . ."

"Great?" Sinclair snarked, leaning against the counter with his arms crossed. Stretched out in front of him like they were, his legs looked a mile long.

His darkness was an odd contrast to Jon—I mean, everything about Eric was dark. The clothes, the attitude. Even the way he carried himself; like he could pounce on you at any minute.

Meanwhile, Jon was practically vibrating from trying just to stand still, and he kept raking his hands through his blond hair, which did nothing to straighten it. He was always in constant motion, while Eric could do statue imitations and win, every time.

Jon's blue eyes watched us all anxiously, but I could smell gun oil and leather, so I knew he was wearing a holster some-where—probably his armpit. Guys loved the armpit holster, though my mom had taught me it was one of the worst places to carry a gun. You could never get to it in time.

And he probably had at least one knife on him. He looked like a corn-fed nineteen-year-old, and he was. But he had also teamed up with a bunch of loners and killed more vampires than most people would see in a lifetime.

Luckily, he liked me, and liking me had ruined his taste for staking vampires. I wasn't sure why, because most vampires were assholes, but I wasn't going to complain. I held out my hand, and Jon shook it with a sweaty palm. "It's nice to see you, too. Is anything wrong?"

"I guess that depends," he replied, glaring over his shoulder at the lounging Sinclair, "on who you ask."

"No, uh, new dead people, though. Right?"

He shook his head. "Nothing like that. Betsy, can I talk to you in private? Maybe in your room?"

"Our room," Sinclair corrected, and smiled when the blood rushed to Jon's face.

"Oh, so you've finally gotten around to moving your stuff in? You've only had two months."

That took care of the smile, I was happy to see, and sure, maybe I shouldn't have said it, but I couldn't stand to see them picking on a kid. It was the fifth grade all over again.

"The queen has many duties," Tina added, her legs scissoring in her lap as she crossed them and looked smug. "I don't think there's time to—"

"Butt out, Tina. And Eric—knock it off. Hello, guest in our happy home?"

"Uninvited guest," Sinclair muttered.

"You wanna go?" Jon challenged. "Because we'll go, partner. Anytime."

"As a matter of fact, I *do* want to go," Sinclair said, straightening up from the counter in a movement so abrupt, even I couldn't see it.

"No, *no*. You guys! Jeez." I turned to Jon, who had a hand out of sight under his jacket. "Don't you dare pull a gun in my kitchen. I'm the only one who can pull a gun in my kitchen. Let's go up." Men! Like rats fighting over a hamburger, I swear to God. "Tell me all about . . . whatever it is. We all wondered where you went after you left."

He was young enough that he didn't feel silly sticking his tongue out at them—but boy, he sure looked silly. Tina rolled her eyes, but Sinclair just stared at him like a snake at an egg. I bit my own tongue, figuring Jon had taken enough shit for one day.

CHAPTER 8

I let him go ahead of me on the stairs, speaking of juvenile actions. I couldn't help it; he had the nicest butt. He favored faded blue jeans and big belts, shitkicker boots, and T-shirts. He looked like an ad for Wheaties.

We had barely gotten to the first landing when he whirled, grabbed my shoulders, and burst out, "Betsy, you can't!"

Startled, I grabbed his wrists. "What?"

"You can't marry *him*."

"That's why you're here?" I mean, liking me was something, but for heaven's sakes.

"You can't do it, Betsy." I was gently trying to loosen his fingers from my shoulders, but he clung like plastic wrap. "I know you, and it'll never work. You're good, and he's *not*. He's totally not. You can't marry him."

"Jon . . ." My God, was I going to have to break his fingers? "Personal bubble, Jon."

He let go. Whew. "Sorry."

"Jon, listen. I know Sinclair has done his share of—"

"Murderous disgusting blood-sucking deeds?"

"—uh—questionable errands, but he's not really that bad. I mean, Nostro was bad. Monique was bad. He's just trying to get along."

"Betsy, that's the dumbest thing I've ever heard. *He is a bad man.* If this was a western, he'd be the one wearing the black hat."

"Jon, you have no idea what bad really is," I said, as nicely as I could. "If you did, you'd know Sinclair wasn't it. The vampire world, like our world, isn't black and white . . . there's tons of gray areas. Sometimes you have to make a bad choice to do a good thing. He's done everything for me—he's been killed for me, and he's saved my life. I think he's saved my life. I mean, assuming I could even—never mind, we're getting off the subject."

"Betsy." Jon stuck his hands in his front pockets, past the wrist, and looked away. "Sometimes a guy will do things for a—for a pretty girl. I'm not saying I don't think he, uh, likes you."

"You're saying I'm too good for him."

"Well . . ."

"That's really nice." I meant it. It was the compliment of

the month. It was the thing I would take out and reminisce about when I was an old lady. "But I know what I'm doing. And I love him. I bet that's the last thing you want to hear, but it's true. And how could I *not* get married to the guy I love?"

He winced and still wouldn't meet my eyes. "Maybe it's a trick."

"Like a vampire mojo thing? I only think I love him? I really only love his teeth and his dick?"

That did it; he glared at me, full in the eyes, and the blood rushed into his cheeks. "Don't talk like that. That's not what I—"

"Because, believe me, I resisted the dark side for as long as I could. Then I realized he really wasn't. Bad, I mean. Well, that bad." Did it sound like I was making excuses for him? I didn't mean to. It was just . . . difficult to put into words. How I felt about him. What he meant to me. Shit, I'd only admitted to myself that I loved him three months ago. "He just took a little getting used to."

"Betsy, I'm not saying I don't think it's a good match— although I don't."

Now I was confused. "So you *are* saying you don't think it's a good match? Right?"

He kept going, unfortunately. Full speed ahead, and damn the torpedoes. "I don't think he's a good *man*. For anybody."

"Oh, so if he was marrying, say, Tina, you would have come down here to warn her off, too?"

Stubborn silence.

"Jon, did you really come all the way from the valley to try to stop my wedding? Because you had months to do that, you know."

"Ani stopped by and she—we caught up on current events, I guess you could say. And—" He cut himself off, but I knew where he'd been going. *And as soon as I heard you were getting married, I got in my dad's truck and left.* Oh, boy. Poor Jon. Crushes were the absolute worst. I'd almost rather die again. It *felt* like dying again, when you heard the person you adored above all others had never, ever given you a thought like that, and probably never would.

"I'm getting married, Jon. On"—for an awful moment I couldn't remember the new date—"September 15. I'd love it if you could come. All the Bees are welcome."

He smiled. Well, his lips moved. We both pretended not to notice that his eyes had filled and he was sniffing like he'd instantly picked up a cold—or a cocaine habit. "That stupid name."

"Hey, you want to talk stupid? How about the Blade Warriors? I feel ridiculous even saying it to you. You're lucky I just use the first letter."

The Blade Warriors! Oh, boy. Like my life wasn't silly enough. This past summer a bunch of kids—yep, that's right, not one of them could legally drink—got together and started hunting down vampires. The scary part? They were weirdly successful. (Vampires were notoriously complacent.) The scarier part? I was able to talk them into not doing that anymore. The Bees (I tried not to use the stupid name) had scattered and gone their own way. And now one of them was back, almost literally in my lap.

"I don't know if I'll be able to come," he said, changing the subject . . . but not really.

"Well, either way. I'm just happy to have anyone there who has a pulse."

"Will there be a lot of vampires there?"

"Yes, and no. My wedding is not a research opportunity, get it? Throw rice and drink. No, you're too young to drink. Throw more rice. Have a Shirley Temple. Go crazy."

"So it's going to be a *wedding* wedding?"

"Sure."

He chewed on that one for a few seconds. "I've never heard of that before."

"Well, don't you start. Sinclair gives me enough grief."

He perked up. "Really? He doesn't like all the bells and whistles?"

"Oh, you know. He says because we're consorts there's no need for bouquet, maid of honor, best man toast, all that."

"Really?" I could see his dimples again. Odd, the things that depressed the boy and brought him back up. "You, uh, you need any help?"

"You mean planning? Or in general? Because the answer to both is, I dunno. September's a long way off."

"Well . . ." He looked around the foyer and then glanced down the stairs. "I don't have to be back right away . . ."

"Do you have a place to stay?"

"Not really. I was going to stop by the church, see if Father

Markus could put me up for a few nights . . ."

"Is that supposed to be a hint? Because it sucks. Why don't you just shove me off the landing? It'd be more subtle."

He laughed. "Yeah, it was pretty lame. Can I crash here?"

"Of course you can. We've got more rooms than the Hilton." In my mind, I could already picture Sinclair's reaction. I probably wasn't going to get laid tonight, at the very least.

Well, tough shit. The kid had had a rotten enough day; I wasn't going to turn him out onto the street on top of all that.

"That's great. I'd—I'd really like to stay here." He glanced around the ancient staircase. "It looks interesting. Like something out of an old book."

"Yeah, interesting. Hope you like dust. But listen, we've got a feral killer vampire living in the basement, so don't go down there. Oh, and if you drink all the milk, you have to replace it."

"What?"

"I know, but see, we all like milk in our tea, and when we're out it's really—"

"Did you say *feral* killer vampire?"

"Right, right. But he's okay. Just stay out of the basement. I don't want you up to any of your old tricks."

"Anything else?"

"Yeah. Good to see you."

"Good to see you, too." He smiled at me like he meant what he was saying.

Damn dimples.

CHAPTER 9

I tiptoed down the hall and quietly rapped on the door to Sinclair's closet room. It would have been his bedroom, except he didn't sleep in there; he slept with me. But all his clothes and such were in here. And I'm sure that meant something, but I wasn't going to worry about it now.

"Eric?" I whispered, knowing full well he could hear me. But I wanted to keep our impending chat as private as I could.

"Yes?" he whispered back.

"Can I come in?"

"Why?"

I spun around. He was in the hallway, grinning and carrying a foot-thick freshly wrapped pile of clean dry cleaning by the hangers. *Wooden* hangers. Wherever he went, it cost a friggin' fortune. "You know I hate, hate, *hate* when you sneak up on me. You know that, right?"

"It's possible you might have mentioned it once before." He leaned past me and opened the door and then courteously stood aside so I could go in. "What nasty business have you been involved in since we parted ways four hours ago? I can't imagine what else would bring you to my room. Have you finally given in to your primal urge to kill Antonia?"

"I wish."

"Perhaps you kidnapped Baby Jon for his own good, and now you're here to tell me I'm a new father."

"I really wish." I paused. Best to just get it over with. "I invited Jon of the Bees to move in with us."

He was taking each dark suit out of its plastic cocoon and carefully examining it before hanging it on some kind of weird suit tree, and in the middle of the ritual he laughed. "What a coincidence. I invited the new pope for breakfast."

"No, really."

He glanced at me and frowned. It was a mild frown, but pretty much all the sun and joy were sucked out of the room when his smile went. "Elizabeth."

"I know, I know."

"Elizabeth. You didn't."

"I really kind of did."

His eyebrows had rushed together to become one overpowering, disapproving unibrow. "Well, I am sure, since the invitation came so easily and thoughtlessly tripping off your dulcet tongue, you can un-invite him just as easily."

"It's only for a little while. Just till he gets his shit together."

"Oh, so twenty years, then?" he snapped. He tried to stomp toward me, but dry cleaning bags were everywhere and he was momentarily snared. I chewed on the insides of my cheeks and stared at him with wide eyes as he stumbled toward me. *Don't laugh don't laugh don't laugh.*

His black eyes narrowed, and he stomped an errant bag, which deflated with a sad *whooooooooooffff*. "Are you smiling, girl?"

"No, Eric." Girl? That was a new one. "Listen, I could hardly turn him out into the street."

"Why not, exactly?"

"Eric! Come on. Look, I'll make it up to you."

"Too damned right you will," he muttered, and grabbed me by the elbows.

"You're just going to fuck me, right? You're not going to make me run a lint brush over all your suits or anything horrible like that, right?"

"Be quiet." He pulled me in for a savage kiss and then tossed me on the bed and landed on me like a cat. In a flash, one hand was up my skirt, divesting me of my tights, and the other was pulling at his own pants. And while he was busy with all that, his tongue was busy in my mouth. I tried to help, to move, but he was controlling everything, and so I lay there and, as they say to do, thought of England. Except I was really thinking about his big dick and drooling at what he was going to do to me with it.

He pushed inside me and I wasn't ready, but I didn't give a ripe damn. We both grunted as we tried to force friction where there wasn't much. He had stopped kissing me and had buried his face in my throat, and my legs were wrapped around his waist. His shirt was still buttoned, and we both had our socks on.

He finally slid all the way home and I was able to pump back at him, and we found a sort of rhythm. It was better, much better, *way* better—it was *fantastic*. I loved the way his hands felt on my body, strong and frantic, and the way his voice sounded in my head:

Never let anyone else never never you're mine mine mine mine MINE MINE.

Pretty much just frantic. Then he stiffened against me, and even though I was miles away from coming, I didn't mind. I knew he'd spend the next hour making it up to me.

He collapsed over me with a groan, and I laughed; my shirt was still on, too. But with scattered clothes and all the plastic bags, the room looked like Filene's Basement on the day of a really good sale.

"Don't laugh at me, you horrible woman," he said without heat.

"Sorry, Eric. That was a real good lesson you taught me. Consider me chastened. Also, the Minnesota Vikings are moving in tomorrow."

He groaned again. "You're trying to kill me. You should feel deep shame."

"Ha!" I looped my legs around his waist and tickled him

behind his ear, in a spot I knew was sensitive. "Ready to go again?"

"Kill me," he mumbled, slowly unbuttoning his shirt, but he couldn't hide the gleam in his eyes, or the sudden, ah, surge of interest. "The state of Minnesota frowns on premeditated murder, you know."

"The state of Minnesota would frown on pretty much everything that goes on in this house." I pulled off my strawberry socks and threw them in the air. "Let's ride, partner!"

"They probably don't think much of suicide, either," he snarked, but then he was kissing me again, and I pretty much lost the rest.

"What are you supposed to do again?" Jessica whispered.

"I told you, like, three times. Jeez, tune me out much?"

"There's a lot of trivia in your life I have to sift through."

"What am I, the six o'clock news?"

"Exactly!" she said, refusing to take offense. "Sometimes it's hard to remember what's important and what's not so much."

"Very nice! Here . . . one-ten, one-eleven, one-twelve." We paused outside the closed door, which, like all nursing home doors, tried to look homey with cards and such, and was anything but. No matter what you did to them, they looked, felt, and smelled like hospitals.

I rapped gently and, when there was no response, pushed on the door. It wheezed open on pneumatic hinges, and I could see an old lady sitting on the edge of the far bed.

She smiled when she saw us, her gums looking just like Baby Jon's.

"Uh, hi," I said, creeping in like a thief, Jessica right behind me. "I'm Betsy. This is Jessica."

She cupped a hand over one ear. She looked like just about every old person in Minnesota I'd ever seen, which was to say white-haired, blue-eyed, skinny, and wrinkly. She was wearing those old-lady panty hose that rolled to the knees and a faded yellow housecoat, buttoned to her neck.

"Hmm?" she asked.

"I said . . ." I inched closer. The door sighed shut behind us. Thank goodness. A scrap of privacy. "I'm Betsy, and this is Jessica."

"Hmm?"

Oh, great. I leaned over until we were kissing distance. She smelled strongly of apple juice. It brought back awful memories of my candy-striper days. And God knew what I smelled like. Probably the Angel of Death. "Annie sent me!" I bawled. "She said to tell you—!"

She leaned closer. Now we were a fraction of an inch away from *actually kissing*. "Hmm?"

"Annie said to tell you there never was a map!" I screamed, ignoring Jessica's giggles. Great! Maybe some of the nurses on the first floor hadn't heard the first part of this extremely private conversation. *"But there was an account, and here's all the info you need to get into it!"* I handed her a folded piece of paper.

"No se . . ." She shook her head. *"No se, no se."*

"Oh, for fuck's sake." I resisted the urge to kick the bed through the window. "Annie never mentioned *this*."

Jessica was actually lying on the other bed, holding her stomach, in hysterics. "Louder, louder! *No se!*"

"Will you get off your ass and help me, please?"

"I took French. You know that."

"Thanks for a big fat goose egg of nothing. You are, without a doubt, the worst sidekick in the history of duos. Now what?"

Luckily, the old lady—gad, I had to remember she was a person, she had a name (Emma Pearson)—she wasn't "the old lady." Anyway, while I was bitching at Jessica, Emma had unfolded the piece of paper I'd handed her, and her face broke into a huge toothless smile. She said something excitedly in Spanish—I'd only had a year of it in high school and all I remembered was *dónde está el baño?*—and clutched my hand.

"Oh, *gracias,*" she said. "*Muchas muchas gracias.* I am thanking you so much. Thank you."

"Uh . . . *de nada.* Oh, I almost forgot . . . Annie is very, very sorry she stole the money, and she hopes you have a lot of fun with it. She's . . . uh, *lo siento.* Annie *es muy muy lo siento para . . .* uh . . . *para* stealing? *El dinero?*"

Emma nodded, still smiling. I prayed she had the faintest idea what I was talking about. If she didn't, Annie'd be paying me another little visit.

Then we just looked at each other. To break the newly awkward silence, I asked, *"Dónde está el baño?"*

She gave complicated directions, which was okay because

I didn't have to go anyway, and we left after much waving and shouted good-byes.

"She didn't appear to get a word of that," Jessica observed, pulling her checkbook out of her purse, groping for a pen, and scribbling something. "But she seemed to know about the account."

"Maybe she reads more English than she speaks. Or maybe she understands the words *First National Bank* and her own name."

"Maybe." She ripped off the check—I saw it was for $50,000—and casually dropped it into the suggestion box on our way back to the car. "This place really needs new wall-paper. Who picked mucous green?"

"You're asking me? This place is like my worst nightmare. Look at all these poor guys. Shuffling around and just pretty much waiting to die."

"There were some people in the game room," Jess said defensively. "They looked like they were having fun putting the big puzzle together."

"Please."

"Okay, it sucks. You happy now? I wouldn't want to end up here, I admit it."

"A problem you'll never have, honeybunch."

"Well, that's true. And neither will you."

I cheered up a little. No, one thing that was most defi-nitely not in my future was spending my last days scuffing along in Wal-Mart slippers and eating applesauce.

"You remember that time you volunteered at Burnsville

Manor in high school, and you only lasted a day because that old guy punched you in the knee when you tried to make him finish his—"

"Let's stop talking for a while," I suggested, and the cow had the giggles all the way back to the mansion.

CHAPTER 10

"I'm sorry, I'm sorry," she gasped, *ten minutes later*. I couldn't believe she was still hee-hawing about ancient history. "It's just, you went there with such high moral intentions, and you didn't even last a single shift. And you limped for a week!"

"Rich people should never criticize the working class," I snapped.

"Hey, I work fifty hours a week at The Foot."

Dammit, she was right. It had always been something of a mystery to me why she bothered. She pretended like the nonprofit was a tax shelter and she needed the break every April 15, but we all knew it was a lie. Bottom line was, she liked going there, liked seeing her dad's money teach welfare moms how to program computers and get good jobs.

She ran the place with an ever-shifting staff, and me. I did the books when she was between office managers. I didn't much mind the work, but I didn't live and breathe it the way Jess did.

"She seemed like a nice lady."

"Jess! She didn't say five words to us the whole time. She could be a drooling psychopath for all we know."

"Do you think some of the ghosts are bad guys? And ask you to help other bad guys?"

"Great. Because I didn't have enough awful things to contemplate." Horrible thought! One I immediately shoved out of my head.

"Sorry. It was just an idea. Do you think there *are* any old psychopaths?"

"Sure. They're not all killers, you know. It's a psych problem, like schizophrenia. It's not just the property of thirty-somethings. The ones who don't get caught prob'ly get old like any of us."

"I read somewhere that there aren't nearly as many psychopaths—sociopaths?—out there as the media want us to think. Something like one tenth of one percent of the population is a deviant sociopath."

"Well, good. Like the vampires aren't bad enough. They all seem like psychos to me."

"Tough one to argue," she admitted.

"You're right, though! It seems like every book, movie, and made-for-TV miniseries is about a brave young woman—always a shrink or an FBI agent—tracking down a serial killer who has mysteriously targeted her. Or her family. Or her dog. And she, along with the brave hero, must alone face the threat of the drooling nutjob—"

"*Taking Lives* wasn't so bad."

"Oh my God!" I shrieked, nearly driving into a stop sign. "Worst movie ever! I almost gave up on Angelina Jolie after that one."

"Too cerebral?"

"Oh, yeah, real cerebral. Jolie has sex with a guy who may or may not be the villain." Hmm, that didn't sound like anybody I knew, right? Argh. I shoved that thought into the tiny corner of my brain where I kept all bad thoughts: Prada going out of business, Sinclair coming to his senses and leaving me, me leaving him, the Ant moving in. "Jess, I love you, but—"

"Here we go."

"—you keep your taste in movies up your ass. I'm sorry, but it's true."

"Says the woman who bought *Blade IV* on DVD."

"That was research!"

"Oh, research my big black ass. You've got a thing for Wesley Snipes."

"First of all, what ass? And second, do not." I had pulled into our driveway, and we were just sitting in my Stratus, arguing, when I noticed that in addition to Jon's truck, there was a navy blue Ford Escort in my driveway.

Cop.

Detective Nick Berry, to be exact. I didn't have to see all

the Milky Way bars on the passenger side floor to know, either. He'd had the same car ever since I'd known him.

"What's he doing here?" Jess asked.

I brought my head down so fast on the steering wheel, the car honked. "What now?" I groaned.

"Hmm, someone else who's desperately in love with you stopping by unannounced," Jessica said with annoying cheer. "Must be Tuesday."

"This is a serious problem."

"Oh, will you spare me please? 'I'm Betsy and I'm an eternally beautiful and young queen with the coolest guy in the universe boning me every night, and whenever he gets tired, other guys are lining up to take his place. *Waaaaaah!*' "

I gave her The Look.

"Sometimes," she admitted, "it's hard to empathize with your problems. Like they weren't trampling over me to get to you when you were alive."

"That's not true!" I said, shocked.

"What's more irritating—being invisible, or you not having a clue about your effect on men?"

"Jess, stop it. The last word I'd pick to describe you is *invisible*. You've dated senators, for God's sake."

She dismissed the Democrat with the great hair with a wave of her newly manicured hand. "Fortune hunter."

"Well, that one guy, no kidding. Okay, maybe there were three or four. But I'm just saying, having these guys popping up is a serious problem. And remember—half the time it isn't even me, it's my weird vampire mojo that's bringing them in.

Like they say, just because they don't seem like problems doesn't mean they really aren't. Problems, I mean. For example, I'd like to have your tax troubles—"

"No, you wouldn't."

"Okay, I wouldn't. But I'm just saying. There are things going on in your life that I wish were going on in mine. Like lunch. Chewing. Sunrises."

"I'm usually in bed by then," she confessed.

"Well, you shouldn't be. Enjoy them while you can." It wasn't like me to be so serious about any particular subject, and I think she got it, because she just nodded and didn't make with the jokes.

"Before I get caught up in whatever fresh hell this is, please don't let me forget I'm supposed to baby-sit Baby Jon tomorrow night."

"Jon the Bee, Baby Jon the baby. Like that's not confusing. And don't forget your dad, John the Eternally Annoying."

"Don't give me anything new to worry about, I'm begging you."

"Me? It's not me, honey."

I got out to face the new problem. Maybe Nick was only there to break up my wedding. Sad when that was the cheerful thought I clung to.

CHAPTER 11

"I'm the local liaison for the Driveway Killer task force," Nick explained, fussing with his coffee and finally putting it down on the coffee table in front of him.

"Driveway Killer?"

"The one who's yanking these poor women right out of their own driveways, strangling them, and then dumping the nude bodies in public parking lots?"

"Oh, *that* Driveway Killer." It was embarrassing to admit, but I never watched the news and I never read the paper. Not before I died, not after. (Well, I skimmed the birth announcements, but only since the Ant's eighth month, and never since Baby Jon came squalling into the world.) I mean, seriously. Why bother? It was never, ever anything good. Even in

Minnesota, which had a pretty low crime rate, even here they only wanted to talk about the bad. Only the bad. If I wanted to get depressed, I'd read an Oprah pick.

I mean, I never even checked the weather reports anymore. And I sure as shit didn't watch TV; I was a DVD girl.

So while Nick was looking amazed that I could live in the same state with rampant media coverage (was there any other kind?) of a killer, Jessica was just nodding. My massive ignorance of current events was nothing new to her.

"Yeah, I've read about him."

"Who hasn't?" I asked gamely.

They ignored me, which I deserved. "And you're on the task force?"

"Yeah."

"To catch a serial killer."

"Yeah."

She tried to muffle it, but the laugh escaped anyway. I knew why—what had we just been talking about ten minutes ago? It was ludicrous.

But not to Nick, who was blinking fast and, I could tell, about to ask Jessica just what the hell her problem was. And never mind that she was the richest person in the state.

"It's late," I said. "She's tired. We're all tired. Long day."

"Uh . . . yeah." He checked his watch. "After ten already."

"I'm so sorry," Jessica said quickly. "I wasn't laughing at you, and I wasn't laughing at those poor girls."

"No," Nick lied, "I didn't think so." He turned back to me. "Anyway, Betsy, I'm sorry about it being so late, but I know about the hours you've been keeping lately, so I took a chance and swung by."

"You're welcome anytime, Detective," Sinclair said from the doorway.

Nick, in the act of picking up his cup, spilled his coffee . . . just a bit, but enough to wreck last month's issue of *Lucky*. I sure couldn't blame him; Sinclair was about as noisy as a dead cat.

"Jesus! You scared me. Which is not something we hotshot Minneapolis detectives like to admit," he joked, trying to cover the fact that his pulse had gone from ba-DUMP . . . ba-DUMP . . . ba-dump to BADUMP BADUMP BADUMP BADUMP!

"I apologize. It's Nicholas Berry, right?"

"Nick. Yeah."

Jessica gave me a look while they shook hands and sized up each other. Nick was built like a swimmer—lanky, with lean lines and big feet. His hair was bleached by the sun— he liked to save up and go diving on Little Cayman—and he had adorable laugh lines in the corners of his eyes.

Sinclair was broader and taller, and much older, but Nick had a gun, not to mention youth on his side. So you never knew.

The problem with the polite hand-shaking and "How do you do's" was that they had met before. In fact, Nick had come to me right after I'd risen as a vampire. In a moment of *extreme* weakness, I'd gotten (nearly) naked with him and it had sort of driven him out of his mind.

Sinclair had had to step in and make things right, and had used his vampire mojo to make Nick forget everything about that night. That I was dead, that Nick and I had seen each other (almost) naked, that he'd been a wreck when I wouldn't bite him again, wouldn't eat, wouldn't sleep. Everything.

The problem was (one of the problems), Nick kept popping back into my life at the weirdest times. Tina suspected he knew more than he was telling. And I honestly didn't know either way. But it wasn't exactly something we could come out and ask him.

So we sat around and pretended he didn't know we were vampires. And we didn't know if we were all pretending. Usually Sinclair and Tina could smell a lie from a hundred miles away, but Nick was a cop. He lied for a living.

"I'm Betsy's fiancé," Sinclair was explaining. "Eric Sinclair."

"Oh." Nick's face fell a bit, and Jessica shot me another look. I felt like throwing my tea in my face, just for an actual *physical* problem.

"We're getting married on July 4th."

"September 15th," I said quickly.

"As I said," Sinclair continued smoothly, "September 15. We do hope you can join us."

"Uh, thanks. I'll—thanks." He looked down at his hands for a minute and then back at me. "Anyway. The reason I stopped by. This killer—he's targeting your type."

"He is?" I was beyond appalled. A type? Gross!

"Tall blondes," Sinclair said. "With blue or green eyes."

When we all looked at him, he said, "Some of us read the paper."

"Not that they're hard to come by in Minnesota," Nick added, "and maybe it's just a, you know, coincidence of geographical type, but still."

"What does VICAP say about it?" Sinclair asked.

Nick shrugged. "The feds won't catch this guy, no matter how many forms we feed into the computer. He'll get nailed by good old-fashioned cops."

I hoped Vicap, whoever he was, didn't hear Nick running down the FBI. Besides, that's what they did, right? Catch psychos? Not that I doubted Nick's ability. But I was glad he had help on this one. And really really glad I wasn't involved.

"And I just wanted to tell you to watch your ass," Nick was saying to, uh-oh, me. Time to tune back in. "Don't get out of the car until you've got your keys organized. Don't linger in the driveway, messing with groceries and stuff. *Watch* the driveway. Check the hedges when you pull in. This guy, I'm sure he's snatching them while they're distracted. They don't even have time to hit the horn. Half the time, there were people in the house, waiting for her. So be alert. Pay attention."

"Okay, Nick," I said obediently. It was, of course, ridiculous and sweet at the same time. The last thing I had to worry about was a serial killer. But it was adorable that he'd come by to give me a heads-up.

Unless he was fucking with us because he knew . . .

No, no. That was the way Sinclair looked at the world, like

it was a big ball of mean out to get him. I swore that no matter how old I got, I wouldn't always assume the worst of people. I'd try, anyway.

"Are there any leads?"

"Just between us?"

"Well, us and the *Pioneer Press*."

He didn't smile at my sucky joke. "We've got shit. No witnesses, nobody even out walking his dog. He's really lucky, the asswipe."

"You'll get him," I said helpfully. Rah rah, the cops!

"Yeah, we will, unless he moves on. But he's going to have to slip up first." Nick's laugh lines suddenly doubled, and he stared at the stained magazine on the table. "And for him to slip up . . ."

"You'll get him," I said again. "And it was, I have to say, it was so nice of you to stop by. I appreciate the warning, and I'll be careful."

"Yes," Sinclair said, walking to the doorway in an obvious gesture for Nick to leave. Awkward! "It was very kind of you to stop by and warn my fiancée. I can assure you I'll look after her very carefully."

Now, if anybody else in the world said that, it'd seem loving and concerned. When Sinclair said it, it sounded vaguely like a threat. Certainly it was weird enough for Nick to give him the 'raised-eyebrows tough-cop' look.

Then he got up (reluctantly, it seemed to me) and said, "You just moved to the area, right, Mr. Sinclair?"

"No," Eric replied. I noticed he didn't ask Nick to call him

Eric. But then, except for my roomies, nobody ever did. "I've been here a long time."

"Oh, okay. Remember what I said, Betsy."

"I will, Nick. Thank you again for stopping by."

"Jess, walk me out?"

She looked startled but gamely jumped to her feet. "Sure. You can check the driveway for us."

"Already did," he said, smiling at me, "on my way in."

CHAPTER 12

I had my ear jammed so tightly against the door between the parlor and the hall, I probably had splinters in my cochlea. (It was weird how things like my tenth-grade biology report on the inner ear stayed with me for, like, ever.)

"Thanks again for coming over," Jessica said, sounding resigned. I figure I knew why. Nick was about to hit her up for a contribution to the Policeman's Ball, or whatever. I felt bad—Nick's devotion to me *was* a little on the obvious side—but what could I do? What could she do?

"I was really glad to see you were up this late, too," Nick said. "I've been meaning to talk to you for a couple of weeks, but things—you know. Work."

"Sure," Jess said. "What can I do for you?"

"Well, the captain mentioned he saw you at the new Walker exhibit, and I know you're into that stuff. I don't know if you heard, but—you probably heard—there's a new Matthew Barney exhibit opening this weekend, and I was wondering if you'd want to go."

"That'd be really mmm hmmm hmmm bmmm."

"Quite rude," Sinclair commented.

"Shhhh!"

"Bmmm mmm hmmm mmm?" Shit! They were walking through the house. There were about eight doors between me and the front door.

"Darling, whatever it is, she'll tell you about it the second she returns."

"Yeah, yeah." I turned. Sinclair was in my personal bubble, as usual, looking amused, also as usual. "I was just curious, that's all."

"Nosy."

"Probing," I insisted. "Like a reporter."

He put his hands on my shoulders and picked me up for a smooch. My feet were dangling a good six inches off the floor as I kissed him back, more a distracted peck because I was wondering what the other two were talking about. He nuzzled into the base of my throat but didn't bite, which is about as loving a gesture a vampire can make.

I guess that sounds romantic and all, and it kind of was, but it was hard to just, you know, dangle there. So I oomphed and umphed and climbed him until my ankles were crossed behind his back and my arms were looped around his neck.

"How delightful," he said. "This is bringing something more interesting than current events to mind."

"Perv. Can you believe Nick just stopping by like that?"

Sinclair's mouth went thin. "Yes."

"Wasn't that nice?"

"Yes. Nice."

"Oh, take it easy. Threatened much? Dude, take a break, go look in the mirror, and then relax, okay?"

"I didn't win you only to have you be distracted by some living meat with a shiny badge."

I gaped at him. Okay, I knew Sinclair generally felt vampires were superior to regular guys, but . . . living meat with a shiny badge?

"You didn't exactly win me," was the best I could come up with. "I'm not a Lotto ticket."

At my expression, he added, "You know you're attracted to shiny things. If you were a raven, you'd snatch that badge and go put it in your nest."

"Wh—uh—" Okay. One thing at a time. "Okay, listen, the reason I was trying to hear is, I just—Jessica said the dumbest thing on the way here. How sometimes she felt invisible next to me."

"Who said what?"

"Very funny. Don't you think that's dumb? I thought that was dumb."

"Dumb," he agreed.

I tried to kick him, but my feet were, of course, behind him. "This is serious! A) it's so not true, and b) it's terrible that she thinks that. But I think I know why she's got such a silly idea in her head."

"Because you're the eternally young, beautiful vampire queen no man can resist?"

"No!" Aw. But no. "She hasn't gone on a date in forever; she hasn't had a steady boyfriend since—jeez, when *did* she break up with dave?"

"Elizabeth."

I rested my chin on his shoulder and thought. "Was it before or after my dad threw the Ant the anniversary party at Windows? Because he—dave—came with her for that, but was that their 'we really can just be friends' date? Or were they really still living together then?"

"dave?"

"Yeah, after they broke up we decided he didn't deserve to have a capital letter in his name. Anyway, I need to fix her up. Trouble is, I'm running around with gay guys and vampires."

"That is a problem."

"Ha! So you agree vampires make rotten dates."

"That is a subject for another time. However, I think this could be very, very good for us."

"What?" I felt his forehead. "Are you all right? Because it almost seems like you're not following this at all."

"So we, and by we I do mean you, dearest, need to be supportive."

"What?"

I heard rapidly approaching footsteps, and Sinclair set me

down. So things looked relatively innocent when Jessica burst
into the room and yelled, "Nick asked me out!"

Then, the scowl. "I know you bums were talking about
me."

CHAPTER 13

I recovered quickly. Which is to say, I stammered and mumbled and Sinclair had to totally help me out.

"Can you believe it?" she said gleefully.

"Of course he did, dear. Frankly, I'm surprised there hasn't been a stampede. You are a worthy prize for any man."

She beamed. "Aw, Eric. Let's gloss over how incredibly creepy that is and instead talk about the fact that I have a date."

"I'm surprised that you're surprised," he said.

"If they're rich, they don't try," she explained, "and if they aren't, they're freaked out because I'm rich. That's oversimplifying it, but . . ."

"I know several men who would leap at the chance to see

you in a . . . social capacity," Sinclair said. "Really, dear, what are"—another tiny hesitation—"friends for? You should have mentioned this long ago."

"Well, I dunno. It's hard to set up a friend with a friend . . . it's so awkward if it goes badly."

"Wait a minute!" I cried. "Eric Sinclair! You knew when she came back in the room that—you could hear their whole conversation?"

"This is new?" Jess asked. "You guys all have ears like bobcats. Fucking creepy, is what it is."

"You could have a conversation with me, make out a little, *and* listen in on them, but you can't go meet the florist because you've got a conference call in Paris at the same time?"

"I think the thing to focus on," Sinclair said, "is what Jessica will wear to the opening."

She was actually jumping from one foot to another. I hadn't seen her so excited since she got her tax bill down to six figures that one time. "I was thinking my black Donna Karan."

"No, no. First, every woman there will be wearing the *de rigueur* little black dress."

"Good point," I admitted, momentarily distracted.

"Number two, you have wonderful coloring that you simply must play up."

Jess was hanging on his every word. "Really, Eric?"

"Dear, you've got the cheekbones of an Egyptian queen. You're a Tiger Lily. You have to, and shall, stand out among the drab little Minnesota daisies."

"Hello!" said one of the daisies.

They ignored me. "Eric, that is *so nice*."

"I'm not nice, dear. Now. Back to the matter at hand." He began to pace. I began to wonder why I'd gotten out of bed that night. "You could get away with, say, the orange Tracey Reese."

"Isn't that one backless? You think that'd be okay for the Walker?"

"The Kay Unger poppy print, then," he suggested.

"I must say, Sinclair, you are not afraid of color," I commented, trying to affect a Sinclair tone and failing. "Isn't that the one with the green flowers all over it? Head-sized flowers?"

"Not every woman can wear it," he admitted.

"It cost a friggin' fortune," Jess said, watching him prowl back and forth like a big panther, "so I'd *better* wear it again."

"We must walk a careful line," Sinclair lectured, "between dressing appropriately for your role, but not making Detective Berry feel out of place or inferior. Which, given the disparity in your incomes, will be difficult at best."

I reeled. There were so many things wrong with that statement I hardly knew where to start with the bitching.

"So dress well, but not rich," Jess said, oblivious to the massive wrongness we were in the middle of.

"Exactly."

"Excuse me," I interrupted. "Sinclair, I haven't forgotten about the florist/eavesdropping thing. And you're weirdly interested in Jessica's date, which I've got problems with on about nine different levels. And Jess, I have to say—" What? What the hell was I going to say?

I can't believe Nick asked you out. For someone who was supposedly into me, he sure got over me pretty damned quick. How could you agree to go out with him when you were sure he liked me? I tried to find a nice way to sum up my weirded-outness in one sentence. It was tough work, being an honest friend. "—I haven't seen you this, uh, excited in a long time."

"I haven't dated since way before you died." She hugged herself and spun in a small circle. "And he's *sooooo* cute!"

"Exceedingly cute," Sinclair encouraged. "Quite very much cute."

I figured it out right then. Sinclair never did anything without about nine secret agendas. He wanted a cop on the string. Awfully handy. Of course, it was only a first date, but if things went well . . .

"I thought you didn't go out with white guys," I pointed out. It was a straw, sure, but I was desperate to clutch at anything.

"I thought *you* said that was bigoted, asshole-esque, and twentieth-century."

"Oh, you're going to start listening to me now?" I grumbled. "I'm not saying I wasn't right, but your timing's a little weird."

"Now that that's settled, we have to decide on the appropriate post-gallery activity."

"That's not all we've got to decide on," I muttered and was—surprise—ignored.

"Because Detective Berry did the asking, I think we can

assume he will want to treat you to whatever diversion you select."

"Dude. You are getting *way* overinvolved in this. Do you obsessively plan our dates? Not that we've ever actually been on a date . . ."

"Shut up, Betsy. For just this one time, it's about me. Go on, Eric."

"So it must be something you both like, that will not be terribly expensive, and that will encourage him to see you again in a social capacity, but not be too intimidating or force a false sense of intimacy."

I hitched up an imaginary belt. "That's a tall order, sheriff."

"Dinner anywhere decent is out. So is coming back here for a drink; this house definitely sends a message. Your idea of fast food is Red Lobster, so that lets out activities that are, ah, middle class. Which means . . ."

Jess waited. I waited. What the hell, I was curious. He could write a book. Nobody was good at dating. Everybody liked advice about it.

"Coffee and dessert at Nikola's," he decided after a moment's thought. "The coffee is first-rate, the food is excellent, it won't be terribly expensive if you don't eat a full meal, and the biscotti is homemade."

"*Oooooooh.* Sinclair, you are *it.*"

"Yes," he replied smugly.

"I am so scared right now," I said.

CHAPTER 14

Before I could take Sinclair aside and ream him out for . . .
well, everything, and before I could take Jess aside and get
the real scoop, the doorbell rang.

"Jessica, I would very much like to continue this conversation," he said, "but I must ask you to excuse us."

"Oooooh," she replied. "Vampire biz, huh?" The evening
must be one shock after another, because I hadn't heard this
many *ooooohs* in . . . ever. "Who is it?"

"No one," he said calmly, "I wish you to meet." He inclined
his head toward the door to the stairs. "If you please."

I didn't know what to say, and I could tell Jessica didn't,
either. After an awkward couple of seconds, she shrugged and
trotted out.

"Scream at me for that," he said, walking toward the front door, "later."

I was sort of terrified to see who it was, and as usual, my imagination ran away from me, because it was a perfectly nice-looking (beautiful, really) older woman. She looked like a librarian in her lilac blouse, gray skirt, sensible panty hose, and black pumps. They were leather and unscuffed.

She herself looked to be in her fifties, with black hair streaked with silver, and a handful of laugh lines in the corner of both eyes.

Her eyes.

There was something weird about her eyes. Sinclair had eyes like that, sometimes. When he was pissed at what was going on (read: other vampires trying to kill me), his eyes went like that. They were so black you couldn't see into them, like those sunglasses state troopers wear. You looked in and—it's hard to explain—you only saw yourself. Most times I could see his softer side, his love and worry for me, his amusement, the good stuff. And the times I couldn't see those things, I usually had my hands too full to worry about it.

I stared at her, a little scared, and she bowed and said something in (I think) rapid French.

Sinclair gave her a smile that looked 85 percent real. "Good evening, Marjorie."

"Your Majesties."

"It's good to see you again."

"And you, Sir."

Sinclair bent and kissed her hand, European style, but

before anybody could kiss mine, I stuck it out to be shook. She did, smiling at me, and I almost dropped her hand. She was cold, which I expected, and I couldn't see anything in her eyes but me, which I did not.

An old one, I decided. A vampire who has seen absolutely everything—*everything*. And doesn't give a ripe shit anymore. About anything. I pitied them as much as I feared them. And I felt pretty sorry for them.

"It's nice to meet you," I lied.

She inclined her head. "Majesty. We have met before."

"No, we haven't." I'd never have forgotten those eyes. Not even Nostro had eyes like those. No, we hadn't met. And after today, I hoped we never would again.

"I was in a group that came to pay tribute after Nostro's, ah, accident on the grounds. Perhaps you didn't notice me."

"No, definitely not." Then, because it's possible she was disappointed (but who could tell? she was a damn robot), I added, "Sorry if I missed you in the crowd."

"Quite all right, my queen. Of late you had . . . a full agenda."

I laughed unwittingly. The robot had been programmed to make amusing observations! "That's one way of putting it."

"Something to drink? We have a Chateau Leoville Poyferre you might like."

We did?

"My king, that is as tempting an offer as I've received all year, but I must return to my duties. I only came by to beg the queen a favor."

She did? At least she was speaking English.

"Well," I said, "come on in."

"Thank you, my queen."

To save time, we took the parlor right next to the front hall, and ole Marjie got right to it.

"As you know, I am head of the library downtown."

She *was* a librarian! I pretended like I knew, and nodded.

"I am starting a newsletter for the vampire community."

"You are?"

"It was your idea, my queen. 'Fer cryin' out loud, why don't you guys get a newsletter or something, I mean, cripes.'"

Sinclair grinned. "It has the ring of authenticity."

"When did I say that?"

"On the occasion of our first meeting, which you do not remember."

"Well, excuse me, I might have had a few things on my mind that day! If you don't come right up and introduce yourself, don't bitch about me not remembering you!"

"I apologize again," Marjorie said tonelessly, "for all my shortcomings."

"And you're stealing lines from *Gone With the Wind*!"

At last, the robot loosened up a little. She even smiled a little. "You have seen the movie?"

"Only about eight thousand times. It's not in the book, but it's a great scene . . . the one where Rhett almost gets called out, but he won't fight because he knows he can totally kick everybody's ass, and killing Charles Hamilton would be annoying and a big waste, so he just bows and leaves."

"I think that touches on a rather large theme of the book *and* the movie," Marjorie said thoughtfully, crossing her ankles like a lady. "Because we see Rhett's bad side frequently, but usually we only see his good side in relation to Scarlett."

"Yeah, like when he brought her the hat after the blockades tightened, and stole a horse for her so she could get out of town and see her mom. Who was dead. But Scarlett didn't know that."

Marjie was smiling patiently through my excited interruption. "But here, he has a chance to shoot a man from his own hated planter class, in a way that is societally acceptable, and instead, he—"

"Vamooses to the library, which is where he meets Scarlett and all that other stuff happens."

"Love. Death. War." She sighed. "Those were the days."

I ignored the uber-creepiness of the psycho librarian and went on in the same, uh, vein. "You know, I never thought of it like that! That from the very beginning, he was redeemable."

Marjorie shrugged. "I have been reading that book since the year it was published, and every time, I find something new. Extraordinary!"

Well, shit! Anybody who liked *GWtW* couldn't be that bad. Right? Right. "Listen, I'm sorry we got off on the wrong foot. I'm terrible with names and faces, and I'm sorry I didn't remember you."

"That's quite all right, my queen," she said, and this time it seemed like she meant it. "As I am here to ask a favor, I'm hardly in a position to sulk."

"Yeah, well. Never stopped me. What's up?"

"Well, as I mentioned earlier, I'm the local librarian."

Local library? As in, there was more than one? "Sure, sure. I remember."

Sinclair shot me a look, which I pretended not to see. He hadn't said a word for a couple minutes, but he seemed relieved we weren't going to scratch each other's eyes out.

"And as I said, I will be starting a newsletter. It will be online and only viewable to vampires who have the appropriate passwords, etcetera."

"You're not worried about someone hacking into it?"

She smiled thinly. "No."

"Right. Okay, go on."

"I would like you to contribute to it, my queen."

"Contribute . . . you mean, like write something for it?"

"Yes, ma'am. Every month."

"But . . . come on, Marjie—"

"Marjorie." Sinclair and Marj corrected me simultaneously.

"—you must have a million people who can do this for you."

"That is not the issue, my queen. As you of course have discovered yourself, many of our kind are having, ah, difficulty accepting your new . . . position."

"That was supertactful."

Another tiny smile. "Thank you, my queen. I feel, and

many of my counterparts concur, that this would be a way for the community to get to know you. Perhaps come to appreciate the . . . finer qualities that aren't, ah, immediately apparent."

"Wow." I was shaking my head in total admiration. "You should work for the United Nations. Seriously. I mean, when *he* tries that stuff, I just get pissed."

Ole Marjie inclined her head modestly. Sinclair gave me a look but still didn't comment.

"What would you want me to write?"

"Oh, whatever you wish. Neighborhood observations, essays on the eternal struggle between man vs. vampire, the pros and cons of keeping sheep—"

"I've got it!"

"Ah, the sheep issue. I admit, it can be controversial—"

"Shut up about the sheep, Marj." Sinclair winced, but I didn't give much of a shit. "No, I'm going to do a Dear Betsy letter. What's the one thing I've wished I could have since I woke up dead?"

"A sheep?"

"Marjorie, enough! No, I wished there was someone I could ask about vampire stuff and I'd get the straight shit in return. Not political shit, not 'oh, it's okay if you kill people as long as you're aligned with so-and-so' stuff. *Real* stuff. It'll be a 'Dear Betsy' column. Ann Landers for vampires!" As Jess would say, *"Oooooooh!"* I could hardly sit still, I was so excited!

Sinclair was rubbing his eyes. Marjorie looked at him for

help and, correctly guessing none was forthcoming, looked back at me. "Ah . . . my queen, I admit I had a more, ah, *scholarly* approach in mind . . ."

"Then boy, did you come to the wrong house. I didn't even finish college."

"Oh."

"I bet you did, though."

"I have fourteen Ph.D.s."

"Geek, huh?" Ack! Fourteen! No wonder I got her mixed up with a robot. "Anyway, back to me. When do you need my first column?"

"Ah . . . whenever you wish. The newsletter will be published on your schedule, of course, and—"

"I'll have it for you by the end of the week. There's not a moment to lose! Just think, there's new vampires walking around right this second who don't have a clue how to act!"

"And you will infect them all."

"What?"

"I said, it sounds like we'll have a ball. I shall go back to the library at once and . . . prepare."

"Great!" I jumped up. Sinclair slowly stood, like an old, old man. Marjorie stood the same way; it was weird. They both looked crushed and knowing at the same time.

He kissed her hand again. "Thank you."

"My king, I only do my duty."

"For coming by."

"Sir, I am your servant."

"Yeah, thanks," I butted in, because I had the weird feeling they weren't talking about what I thought they were talking about. "Send me your e-mail address, and I'll zap the column over to you in the next few days. I'm TheQueen1@yahoo.com."

Was that a shudder? Naw. My imagination was working overtime. And speaking of overtime, I could hear Marc park his shitbox car and come bounding up the walk. How he kept his energy after fifteen hours on his feet in the E.R. was beyond me.

He popped the front door open and spotted us in the entryway. He covered the distance between us with half of one of his characteristic long lopes, and his green eyes brightened. "Hi, guys!"

I was torn. On the one hand, as he was generally a depressed individual with big problems (gay, dying father, premature balding), I was always happy to see him happy. We had met when he was moments from throwing himself from the top of the hospital at which he worked too many hours. I talked him out of jumping and took him home. He'd been hanging out with us ever since. And in the past few months, he'd had his dad set up at a great private—I guess it was a hospice, except it was a private home, and the nurse who lived there only took care of three people. So it wasn't like being stuffed in a nursing home. Anyway, he'd gotten his dad squared away and visited him as often as he could stand (I guess it was kind of a strained relationship), he'd gotten a new boss at work, he was growing out his hair, and he'd had a date in the last five weeks.

On the other hand, I wanted him nowhere near Marjorie.

Marc was like a puppy around vampires . . . had no clue how totally friggin' dangerous they really were.

"So what's doing? What are you guys up to? What's going on?" Arf, arf, sniff, sniff, sniff.

Marjorie's delicate nostrils flared. "Your pet smells like blood."

"Yeah, kid fell out of his tree stand and bonked himself a good one," Marc said cheerfully, ignoring—or not hearing—"pet." "Bled all over me. I had to get a new scrub top, but man, do I need a shower. Hi, by the way," he added, sticking out his hand. "I'm Marc Spangler. I live here with Betsy and Eric."

She looked at the hand like he'd offered her a dead garter snake, and I could feel my eyes widen, practically bulge in their sockets. I got ready to rip her a new asshole—what was it with old vampires and being so shitty to regular people?—when Sinclair's hand clamped over mine . . . hard.

I yelped just as Marjorie decided to shake Marc's hand. "You live here with them?" she asked.

"Yup," he replied cheerfully. "It's not home, but it's much. Olivia Goldsmith wrote that, by the way."

"Mmmm. She's the one who died of liposuction, yes?"

"No," he corrected. "She died of complications after lipo."

"I see. If you live here with them, why do you go to a job?"

"Uh . . ." He actually thought it over for a couple seconds. "Because I'm not a two-legged parasite?"

"Mmmm." She caught the neckline of his scrub top and

pulled; with a squeak, he bent down to her. He had a foot and thirty pounds on her, but she manhandled him (no pun intended) easily, like he was a mannequin made of feathers. "But you *haven't* been bitten," she said to his neck. "Yet. Mmmm . . ."

I opened my mouth. *Take your fucking hands off him NOW* was already in my head and trying to rush out of my mouth when Sinclair squeezed again. I groaned instead; I could feel the little bones in my hand grinding together. He wasn't hurting me, but I sure wouldn't want to spend a day doing that.

"Marjorie, don't you have business to be about?" he asked calmly.

Totally distracted, she looked up, and I was shocked to see her fangs had come out. "Eh? Oh." It was obvious, when she let go and Marc popped back upright, that she was massively disappointed. "Yes, of course. Forgive me. I haven't dined yet this evening, and it's made me forget my manners. I will take my leave."

"Nice to meet you!" Marc chirped. And as she bowed and then let herself out the front door, I looked at Marc and saw it: he didn't remember the last minute. He'd had no sense of being in danger, no sense of inappropriateness or cruelty from Marjie. As far as he was concerned, he'd met a nice older lady on his way in, and now he was going to grab a shower.

"I think I'll go grab a shower," he said. "Later, guys."

I started to have a dim idea why Sinclair had a) gotten rid

of Jess, b) been polite under extreme provocation, and c) didn't let me hang myself.

"I hope you took a good look, dear," he said, listening to the car drive away. "Because that is the oldest vampire you're likely to ever meet."

"She's an asshole."

He shrugged. "She's old. It's . . . difficult to surprise her. You did, though." He smiled, and it was like the sun coming up on the last day of winter. "You did very well."

"It's hard to hate anyone who has such good taste in movies. Though if she'd put another hand on Marc, I would've had to bring down the spank."

He got this weird look on his face, like he was horrified but wanted to laugh, too. "You—you must not. Or, if you decide, you must discuss it with me first. Never touch her alone. Never, understand?"

"Okay, Sinclair. Because that's *sooooo* me. Maybe we can form a committee and vote on every single thing."

His eyes went narrow but he hung onto the smile. "Listen, please. She is old, as I have said, and she has many friends. Friends she made herself, if you understand my meaning. She is . . . I guess you would say she is set in her ways. The old ways."

"Yeah, I get it. She's old; she's a stubborn jerk; she thinks humans are moronic lunch boxes; she's got a million friends; and if she doesn't like me, she could cause a lot of trouble for me."

"Us," he corrected. "It's important to keep Marjorie and

those like her on our side. When I went to Europe last
fall . . ."

He'd never talked about the trip much. Brought me back
a nice present and mentioned he'd met up with friends, and
that was that. "Yeah?"

"Let's just say I was dismayed by how many vampires were
not on our side."

"Yeah, but you fixed it, right? You always fix everything.
Like tonight. And ow, by the way." I flexed my hand, which,
if I'd still been alive, would have been throbbing painfully.
"Next time just wave a hand puppet at me, willya? I *need*
this hand."

"To write your 'Dear Betsy' column."

"Was that an eye roll?" I demanded. "Are you rolling your
eyes at me, Eric Sinclair?"

"Oh, no, beloved. I would never so disrespect my queen."

I laughed. "You're so full of shit your eyes are brown."

"They *are* brown," he admitted, taking me in his arms. He
kissed me for such a lovely long time, I forgot about Margaret.
Marjie. Whoever.

"This really isn't the time or place," I muttered into his
mouth as he lowered me to one of the phenomenally uncom-
fortable couches in the parlor.

"I'll have ample notice if someone is coming," he said,
pulling open my blouse and yanking my pants down to my
knees.

"What if I'm the one coming?" I teased, caressing the
bulge in his trousers.

He groaned. "Don't do that unless you want to be finished before we start."

"Eric, you're talking like a man who's being neglected."

He braced himself over the couch, unzipped his fly, pulled my panties aside, and slid into me, neat as a magic trick. "I am neglected," he murmured in my ear. "Whenever I'm not inside you, I'm neglected."

"That's really lame," I whispered back. I braced a heel on the couch arm and met his thrusts. "And we're gonna break this couch."

Fuck the couch.

That thought—cool and uncaring, but hot at the same time—pretty much did me in; I heard something crack in the couch and then I was coming, clutching at Eric while his voice ran through my head, a vivid whisper of longing.

O my own my Elizabeth my Queen I love love love love . . .

I hope he "loved" fixing couches, because that was probably next on our agenda.

He groaned and collapsed over me, which elicited a groan of my own. "Kill me," he mumbled. "I'm an old man, and you're trying to kill me."

"Hey, this wasn't *my* idea, pal. And you're still in your prime. Your immortal dead guy prime." I giggled.

"Are you laughing at me, darling?"

"No, Eric," I said gravely, biting my lower lip so I wouldn't do it again.

"It would crush my tender emotions to know you were laughing at me during this vulnerable time."

"I'd never do that, Eric. So what was it like, inventing the telegraph?"

He chased me up the stairs, and I made a mental note to have someone take a look at that couch later in the week.

CHAPTER 15

It was about five A.M., and I was getting ready for bed (finally! what a long, weird day) when there was a brisk rap-rap at my bedroom door.

"Come on in," I called, buttoning the last button on my new jammies. Aw, they were so soft, so sweet to the touch . . .

Jessica opened the door and stuck her head in and then groaned when she saw me. "Jeez, Betsy! I'll buy you friggin' decent pajamas, okay? You don't have to wear those pieces of shit."

"What?" I cried. "These are brand-new."

"Yeah? What's Sinclair say about them?"

"What part of 'brand-new' aren't you getting? He hasn't seen them yet."

"He sees those, the wedding's off."

"Oh, shut the hell up." I stepped to the mirror and admired the navy blue flannel and red polka dots. They were too long in the pants and arms (I'd found them in the men's section, where I frequently shopped because I was so fucking tall), but a few washings should take care of that. And they were *warm.* "You didn't come up here to critique my nightwear. At least I hope you didn't. Because, really, how lame would that be?"

"No, I sure didn't. But I could sure spend half the night doing it."

"This from someone who wears football jerseys to bed."

"Totally different thing."

"I think I liked it better when you weren't talking to me."

"Too late now. Listen, I wanted to catch you before you guys went to bed—where *is* Sinclair?"

"He made a beeline for the computer after ole Long in the Tooth and 'Tude left."

"Huh. He used to practically count the seconds before you went to bed so you guys could do it."

"We already did," I admitted, "after Maggie left."

"Yet another room you defiled. And Maggie would be the vampire he didn't want me to meet?"

I shuddered. "Don't bitch, J. He was right. She's creepy. She's got eyes like a doll's."

"Barbie Doll or American Girl?"

"Blank." I gestured to my face, trying to convey in five words or less how creepy the woman had been. "Shiny."

"Shiny?" I could see Jess was trying not to laugh. She'd never met Nostro. In fact, I was the baddest vampire she'd ever met, after I'd read the Book of the Dead and gone evil. Which was to say, she'd never met a really bad vampire.

"She almost chomped Marc, and not only did he let her grab him, he didn't remember that she grabbed him. Stay the fuck away, I'm serious."

"Well, if Sinclair's worried about her, that's good enough for me. I've got enough creepy vampires to worry about." She plopped herself into what I always thought of as Marie's Chair. "Listen, are you okay with me going out with Detective Nick?"

"If you're gonna date him, you should probably get in the habit of referring to him just by his first name."

She waved that away. "Yeah, yeah. Are you?"

"Sure. Yeah. It was just a surprise, that's all. A good surprise," I added hastily. "Sinclair's right, somebody should have snatched you up ages ago."

She smiled thinly. "Yeah, well. Nobody's gotten around to it yet."

"I was just thinking that it had been a while for you . . . wasn't dave the last guy you were with?"

She nodded, fiddling with the neckline of her shirt. "Lowercase dave, yup, I remember."

"Okay, then. Look, we know Nick's nice, he's great at his job, he *looks* . . . yum. Go for it. But . . ."

I trailed off because I was torn. Did I warn my best friend that my fiancé was going to do everything in his power to make that relationship work because he was sneaky and that's how he operated? Nick might like Jessica for herself (or not; we hadn't established that yet), but Sinclair liked Nick for his badge.

Or did I keep quiet out of loyalty to my fiancé, the vampire king?

"But . . . ?" Jessica prompted.

"But . . . you . . . should . . . wear clean underwear."

She gave me an odd look. "Thanks for the tip."

"I gotta admit, I was kind of surprised you said yes."

She shrugged and picked a cloth pill off the arm of the chair. She was very fidgety tonight. "I dunno. It's great being with you guys and all, and living here, but the excitement of being best friends with the queen of the vampires doesn't exactly butter my muffin at night, you know? I mean in bed. Because we're all up and running around at night. But you know what I mean, right?"

"Sure. I hope it works out."

"With Sinclair on my side, how can it not?"

"I know! My God, was that weird or what?"

"You boy has a sinister metrosexuality going on," she agreed, "and that's a fact."

"That's one way of putting it. Oh, and get this! I have a job again. I'm writing a column for the new vampire newsletter."

"*What* did you just say?"

"I know!" I plopped down on the bed and propped my chin on my elbows, slumber-party-gossip style. "Can you believe it? Talk about practical. How totally unlike vampires to do something that doesn't involve beheadings or the mass slaughter of innocents."

"Maybe," she suggested, "it'll be an evil newsletter."

"Great. Something new to worry about. Which reminds me—"

There was a tentative knock on my door, one I knew well. "Come in, Jon!"

"Ooooooh," Jessica said, not looking at me. "I forgot to ask you how Sinclair reacted to the news of his roommate."

"It wasn't pretty," I mumbled back. Then: "Hi, Jon! You caught us. Everybody's about ready to turn in."

"Yeah . . . I just got up, actually. This is the one time of day that our schedules actually mesh."

"How interesting," Jess said sweetly, "that you've planned that out already. You've been here . . . what? A day?"

He looked flustered (and adorable!) as he stood in my bedroom doorway, shifting his weight from one foot to the other. "Well, not the one time," he explained. "Because, you know, it's wintertime. So I'll still be awake when the sun starts to go down, and—"

"Jon. My girl has to get ready for bed, and her fiancé's gonna be here any minute. So what's up?"

Not for the first time, I had the impression Jessica didn't much care for Jon.

"I, uh, because I'm going to be in town, I had this idea. Actually, I got it at school. I'm taking a writing class at the U—"

"That'll come in handy on the farm."

"Jessica!" I gasped. What did she have against farmers? "Go on, Jon. We're *all* listening." I glared at her for good measure.

"Well, anyways, I was going to the U last year and then I went back home—"

"Which we already know . . ." Jessica prompted him by making the "speed up" motion.

"—anyway, today I re-registered, and one of my new classes is—well, last year I took a class called The Writing Sampler—and this year I want to focus on the bio class."

"—logy or graphy?" I asked, having trouble seeing where this was going.

"Oh. Biography."

"Is that the one where you write your life story?" I asked, delighted. Yes! Something to keep him busy, and off of me! And off Sinclair's radar, best of all. "What a great idea, Jon! You've lived an incredible life and you're, what? Fifteen?"

"Twenty," he said thinly. "And a biography is when you write about someone else."

"Uh-oh," Jess muttered.

"Oh. Then—oh. Oh! Uh . . ." I blinked rapidly and tried to keep my mouth from popping open. "Well, that's . . . really flattering."

"I think it'd be a great project."

"Jon, you can't write about her and then show it to all your little school chums. We're trying to keep a low profile, here."

"Oh, I know," he said with painful earnestness. "I already told my instructor—"

"You did *what*?" we screamed in unison.

"—that it was fiction. A fake biography about a fictional character. He loved the idea."

Then he's missing the point of the class, I thought but didn't say.

"I mean, come on, you guys. Who'd take it seriously anyway? 'Oh, here's a biography tell-all of a vampire who lives here in the Cities.' Of course he's going to assume it's a fake. In fact," he added proudly, "he can't wait to read it. Said in twenty years of teaching no one's come up with that idea before."

"You didn't come up with it, either!"

He ignored her and looked at me. "So will you do it?"

"Do *what*?"

"Tell me the story of your life."

I opened my mouth.

"No," Jessica said.

I looked at him.

"No," Jessica said. "Bets, I'm doing you the hugest favor of your life here, right now. No. I'm saving you so much trouble right now. From *people*. You know. No."

Jon glared at her. "It's not up to *you*."

"Isn't there a combine you should be changing the oil on?"

"Isn't there a benefit you should be chairing?"

"Come on, guys," I said automatically, thinking.

I knew what Jess was getting at; she was implying that Sinclair would totally flip his gourd. As he sort of had when I told him Jon was staying with us. What could be worse than that?

Aw, Sinclair wouldn't mind. He had more important things to worry about than Jon's schoolwork. Frankly, with vampires like Marjorie running around town, I was kind of surprised he even noticed Jon was here.

And Jon looked so adorably hopeful, so rumpled and sweet in his jeans and yellow "Luke, I'm not your father" T-shirt. And bare feet! My God, you could practically see the straw sticking out of his hair.

"Welllllllllll . . ."

"No."

"Maybe we could try it," I said. "Just to see how it goes. Maybe a couple chapters."

"Nooooooooooooooooo!" Jessica yowled.

That's when Sinclair walked in. "What is going *on* in here?"

CHAPTER 16

"Jon wants to—"

"That was rhetorical; I heard the discussion on the way up the stairs." He strode into the room, put a hand on Jon's face, and shoved. Jessica darted to the door and actually had it open in time for Jon to stumble through it. She took one look at Eric, said, "Good night, guys," and went through the door herself, at a slightly more dignified speed.

"Sinclairrrrrrr!" I yowled. "You can't go around man-handling my friends that way. No wonder he doesn't think I should marry you."

"I know exactly why the infant thinks I shouldn't marry you." He had his back to me, staring at the shelves full of CDs. He'd been sleeping in here for a couple months, but he had yet to move any of his own things in. All his suits and underwear and toiletries (if a vampire needed such things) were in his own room down the hall.

Why had I never wondered what that meant before? That he came to fuck and then left? Unlike me, Eric could move around all day, provided he stayed out of direct sunlight. So I figured, anything was an improvement over all the fighting and massive sexual tension we'd always ever known. And because I assumed after the wedding we'd share a room, not just a bed.

I'd assumed other things before. About Eric. And been wrong.

Worst things first. "You're being a big baby about this. You were a jerk about him staying with us for a while—"

"We are not the Super 8 Motel."

"Says one of the three people who moved in without paying a dime for the place! Or asking me! *I* at least sold my house for the down payment."

"It is childish to pretend it's the same thing," he sniffed. "I was the king, moving to an appropriate domicile to be at my queen's side. Jon is sniffing up your back trail like an addled bull in the pasture."

Wow. He was *really* mad. The farm metaphors only came out when he was superpissed.

"Eric, he's, like, twelve years younger than I am! I'd never go out with someone like that."

He turned away from the wall of Cool. His night attire, I couldn't help but notice, was exceptional: black silk pajama pants. And nothing else. I wished we could quit arguing so I could see if his nipples tasted as good as they looked. "You're sixty years younger than I am."

Nipples be damned! "What?"

"I said, you're sixty years younger than I am."

"Wh—buh—" I honestly never thought of it in terms like that anymore. I used to, when I was a brand-new vampire and he wanted me to choose between him and Nostro, but then I chose, and it's never come up since.

Unless Sinclair thinks it's time to make another choice . . .

"Look, Eric, you're just being . . ." I flapped my hands helplessly. "Well, weird. You're being weird about this. It's you I love. Not Jon. Not Nick."

His eyes narrowed. "What does Nick have to do with anything?"

"I'm just saying! Everyone's so concerned about my love life, nobody's listening to me, to what I want. It doesn't matter how many Bees or cops end up living here; it doesn't change how I feel about you. I made my choice, *you're* who I want to be with. You! The sneakiest, creepiest, studliest guy I've ever known."

He unclenched a bit. "I suppose I must take that as a compliment."

"I don't care how you take it, but be nicer to Jon. Stop shoving him around; it just showcases your—I can't believe I'm using this word in reference to you—insecurity."

"That term is exactly why I haven't yet brought up the subject of your new sleepwear."

"What?" I spread my arms, like Christ on the cross. "You think I'm insecure and that's why I wear this stuff? You're on drugs! Don't you think the dots bring out my high-lights?"

He grinned, started to say something, but then cut himself off and turned back to the wall of Cool.

"How have I not noticed these before?" he asked.

Because we appeared to be done fighting, I didn't say anything, but boy, I was thinking plenty. Like: *well, if you came here for anything but sex, you'd probably notice all sorts of cool things.*

"*Various Hits of the Eighties*. Cyndi Lauper." Sinclair was flipping through the top shelf of CDs. "*Greatest Hits of Duran Duran. All Dance Hits of the Eighties. Eighties, Eighties, Eighties. More of the Jammin' Eighties. Madonna: True Blue. The Pet Shop Boys. The Beastie Boys.*"

"What can I say? I'm eclectic."

"Yes. Eclectic. That wasn't the word that sprang to my mind, I admit."

"Don't tell me you're one of those music snobs." But of course, he was. Nothing in his car but Rachmaninoff.

"No, no. The wedding's off."

"What?"

"I said, you have to take that off."

"Oh." Weird vampire hearing. It was either really good or really bad. "Okay, okay. Do you want to borrow—"

"No!"

"All *right*, don't *yell*." I moodily started unbuttoning my flannel top. "And stop pushing Jon around, I mean literally pushing him. How'd you like it if he put his big ole farm boy mitts on your face and shoved?"

"I would love that," Sinclair replied with scary sincerity.

"Is that the stench of a dead goat I smell, or your testosterone? Cripes, throttle back. Besides, you're missing my point. I'm in here with you, aren't I? I don't go to Nick's place or climb into Marc's bed—I notice you're not weird about Marc—"

"Is that supposed to be a joke? I'd be infinitely more worried about Marc if we were the same suit size."

Hmm, good point. Moving on! "Maybe one of my undead superpowers is to make gay people straight, but I don't see you worrying too much about it."

"No," he agreed, sitting on the edge of the bed and drumming the fingers of his left hand on his right knee. "I don't worry too much about it."

"Right!"

"Also, you are not undressing nearly quickly enough."

"And I'm not in the Bee's bed, wherever that one even is—"

"Second floor. Third one down the hall, right side."

"See? I should be worried about *you* sleeping with him, you're so obsessed."

"Territorial," he conceded. "Not obsessed."

"But it's you I want to be with—did we not figure this all out in October?" I waved my arms, which, as I was unbuttoning, flapped like a clothesline in a windstorm. "It's *your* voice I hear in my head, nobody else's. That should prove you've got nothing to worry about."

"What?"

Oh, fuck.

CHAPTER 17

"Now, don't freak out." Stupid, stupid! I'd meant to tell him, but not like *this*. I was thinking more along the lines of giving him a giant cookie frosted with "I can hear you in my head, lover!" Maybe for Valentine's Day. Twenty years from now.

"What did you say?"

"Okay, it's like this." I hurried over and sat beside him on my—our!—bed, and flung my arms around his shoulders, which wasn't unlike hugging the big oak tree in the back-yard. "When we make love, I can hear what you're thinking. It's in my head."

Nothing. He sat stiffly, like we were playing statues.

I hugged harder. "And the thing is, I've been trying to figure out the right time to tell you, and there just never was one. But now that I see how insec—how worried you are about our houseguest, I figured it would be a good time to *prove* my love and how much we are *meant to be together* because in my whole life and death, I never heard anybody in my head, ever, not one time."

If anything, he got stiffer. "You hear. Me. In your. Head?" he asked carefully.

"Yes. But only during lovemaking. Never before and never after. I mean, I have no idea what you're thinking right now. Although, uh, I can probably figure it out."

"For. How. Long?"

"Since that time in the pool—the first time. And right up until . . . well, earlier. In the parlor, after Margaret left."

"Marjorie," he corrected automatically. He pried my hands off him and pulled my arms away.

"Don't be mad," I said, probably the stupidest line ever, right up there with, "she didn't mean anything to me."

He left.

I sat there and stared at the open doorway. Okay, I knew he wasn't going to take the news well, and I told him in a shitty way. At least I hadn't told him out of spite. But still— he'd had no prep at all. And now he had left, walked out.

I got ahold of myself. I wasn't going to sit on the bed cowering and waiting for him to come back and yell at me, or possibly throw a credenza at me. I jumped to my feet and ran to the door . . . where I promptly smacked so hard into the returning Sinclair I hit the floor like a backhanded pancake.

"Damn," I gasped. "You must have really tooled up those stairs."

"This is no time for one of your amusing pratfalls," he snapped. He stepped over me (he didn't even help me up!) and dropped something big on the bed, something that gave off its own dust.

I was totally horrified to see it was the Book of the Dead.

"Get that thing off my sheets," I ordered. "I just got those last week at Target! They're flannel!"

He ignored me, bent over the book, and flipped through it. Finally (a miracle with neither a table of contents nor an index) he got to the yucky nasty page he wanted, straightened, and pointed.

"What? You want me to . . . forget it, no way. I'm done with that—hey!" He'd crossed the room in a blink, seized my arm, and dragged me over to the Book. "Okay, *okay,* don't *pull.* These are new, too."

I bent over the horrible, horrible thing, written in blood by an insane vampire who could see the future. And never spell-checked, I might add, just to add to the overall fun.

"Okay, here we go—here? Okay. 'And the Queene shall noe the dead, all the dead, and neither shall they hide from her nor keep secrets from her.'" I stood up. "Right, so? We figured that's why I can see the ghosts and nobody else can."

"Keep reading."

"Eric—"

"Read."

I hurriedly bent back to the homework from Hell. "'And shalt noe the king, and all the king's ways, for all their reign o'er the dead, and the king shalt noe hers.' There, cheer up!" I straightened (please God, for the last time . . . no more reading tonight). "See? I know your ways, and you know mine. So . . . I mean, this is deeply meaningful because . . ."

"As you said. You can read my mind during . . . intimate moments."

"Yeah," I nodded. "I told you that. Remember? Told you? As in, didn't keep it a secret?" *For more than eight months?* Shut up, brain.

"I cannot read yours," he pointed out.

"Yeah, I figured," I confessed. "I tried to sort of, uh, feel you out a couple times. But I didn't get anything back."

He just stared at me. I knew that look: penetrating and faraway at the same time. There was some serious thinking going on behind those black eyes.

"Eric . . ."

He took a step back.

"Okay, you're mad. I don't blame you; it was a rotten way to find out. Only, I knew you'd be like this! That's why I was scared to tell you!" Worst. Apology. Ever!

"I am not mad," he said.

"Eric, you're the one I want to be with."

"The Book begs to differ."

"Jeez, we've only been together for two months . . . we've only *known* each other since April. Give me time to 'noe your ways,' dammit, and you need time to noe—know mine.

Just because you can't—you know. Just because you can't right this minute doesn't prove anything. And I'm sorry, okay? I'm sorry I didn't tell you. I wanted to."

"I understand," he said with horrifying distance, "why you could not."

"Eric, *you're* the one I'm marrying!"

"I'm the one you keep changing the date on," he said. "Perhaps because you have realized I am not your equal? Being a soft-hearted wretch, I can see why you would not be up to the task of telling me face-to-face that your feelings had changed."

"That has nothing to do with it!" I screeched. "Oh my God, did you just call me a wretch?" A coward, too! He'd turned telepathy into an excuse to postpone the wedding? Men! "How you could jump to a conclusion like that?"

"Yes, you are correct, it is simply a wondrous coincidence."

"I'm just disorganized, moron! It's not a personal observation! See, see? This is why I didn't tell you, I knew you'd freak out and get pissed."

"I'm not pissed," he said coolly. And . . . he didn't *sound* pissed. He didn't sound like anything I could figure. I didn't know whether to run and put my arms around him, or jump out the window and get away from him. The four feet between us yawned; it could have been the edge of a cliff. "I'm . . . surprised."

He was a liar, that's what he was. Finally, I recognized the emotion. I'd never seen it on his face before, so no wonder it took me a few minutes: it was fear.

Not for me. I'd seen that before, plenty of times. No, this was something else. He was afraid, all right.

Of me.

CHAPTER 18

Dear Betsy,

I'm a new vampire (I was attacked and killed by another vampire while I was on my senior class trip, eight years ago), and I'm not sure exactly of the protocol now. Things were different under Nostro, but I'm not sure how things are with you. There's a girl in my life I "see" once in a while, and she lets me bite her, but she thinks it's just part of fun. Sometimes I'll make friends with a new girl and bite her a few times, too. It's hard because I have to feed every day, but I don't want to kill anyone. Do you have any advice?

Chewin' on 'em in Chaska

Dear Chewin':

Well, you've got the right idea, anyway. Don't kill them, not any of them, if you can help it. They can't help being alive any more than you can help being dead. I try to go out and bite bad guys . . . you know, someone who's trying to drag me into a dark alley to "meet" his friends, someone I catch breaking into my car . . . like that. I feel like they got punished for whatever felony they were attempting, and I got to eat. Try that for a while and see how it works.

If you ever meet that special someone, you could tell her your secret and maybe she could help you out. Also, as you get older, you won't need to feed as much. Cheer up. This, too, shall pass.

"It's pretty good," Jessica said. "Because the newsletter is new, I guess you had to make up the first few questions?"

"Yeah."

"Well, pretty soon you'll start to get real letters, so that's okay. But this isn't too bad."

I started to cry.

"Jeez!" Jessica said, putting the paper down and hurrying over to me. "I had no idea you were such a touchy edit! It's great, it's really great for your first time. Lots of—uh—lots of good advice."

"Sinclair moved out of my room," I sobbed.

"Well, honey, I don't know that he ever actually moved *in*."

I cried harder.

"Uh, sorry. Did you guys have a fight?"

"A big one. The worst one."

"Worse than when you thought he was putting the moves on your sister?"

"I wish that's what it was," I wept.

"Okay. Is it something you can tell me about?"

"No," I sobbed. Sinclair's humiliation was still fresh; the last thing I was going to do was spread it around.

She had poured a fresh cup of tea for me—we were in the kitchen—and now sat down in the chair next to me. My feeble letter lay on the table between us. I'd been desperate to distract myself from the fight. Thus, Dear Betsy.

"Well, honey, is it something bad you did?"

"I didn't think so. I thought it was good. Proof of something good. But he didn't agree. And then he left. It's been two nights, and he hasn't been back; I haven't even seen him in the house. I've seen George the Fiend more than my own fiancé."

"Right, but . . . you're not going around killing Girl Scouts or anything, right?"

I shook my head. "Nothing like that."

"And you didn't read the Book . . . Betsy!" she nearly screamed at my feeble nod. "Did you turn evil again?"

"I wish. I only read the paragraph he made me. He was just making a point. And then he slammed it shut and took it away, and took himself away, too."

"Well, is it something you can say you're sorry for?"

"I don't think I can apologize for this. Besides, I already did. We were pretty mad, though. He might not have noticed. But it was a secret for a long time. I guess I can apologize for not telling him right away."

"That's a start, right?"

"He's afraid of me now," I practically whispered.

Jessica burst out laughing. She laughed so hard she actually slapped the table with her palm. "Scared! Sinclair! Of you!" Slap, slap. "Oh, that's a good one." She sighed and wiped her eyes. "Tell it again; I needed that."

I glared. "I'm serious, Jessica. The thing I told him made him be scared of me. In the past he thought it was cool that I could do things other vampires couldn't—"

"And let's not forget, he wasn't above using you to get what he wanted," she pointed out, her cheeks still shiny from laugh-tears.

"Yeah, I know. But he was never, you know, *scared* of the things I could do. Just . . . impressed, like. He thought they were neat, and he thought it was great that I killed Nostro and what's-her-name, and he thinks it's great that the devil is my sister's mother, but he was never afraid *of me*. I'm telling you. That's what's happened now."

"This thing—whatever it is—it's made him scared of you."

I rubbed my eyes (pure force of habit; I had no tears) and nodded.

"Okay, so you should apologize for keeping the secret and then you gotta wait for him to get over his bad self."

"Wait?"

"Honey, have you *seen* the man? Does he strike you as the type of fellow who's scared of anything, much less his own girlfriend? He's gonna need some serious time to get used to the idea."

"Wh—how much time?"

"You're immortal," she pointed out. "What's the rush?"

"But . . . wedding stuff. We've got to plan the wedding. I can't do it by myself."

"So postpone it again."

"I can't," I said, appalled all over again. "Oh, I just can't. He's got it in his head that—never mind. But one thing I absolutely can't do is cancel it. Full speed ahead on all wedding prep."

"Are you *sure* this horrible thing you've done, it's not evil? What am I saying, it's Sinclair. Evil doesn't scare him. He probably gets off on it, in his heart of hearts."

"Trust me. It's not evil." *Elizabeth, oh my Elizabeth . . . you are sweet, you are like wine, you are . . . everything. I love you, there's no one. No one.* Probably never hear that again, so get used to the mental playback, babe. "It's the total opposite of evil. I thought . . . I thought it was kind of wonderful. But he—he—"

I cried some more. It was lame, but I couldn't stop. Just when I thought that the *one* thing I could count on was Sinclair by my side no matter what happened . . .

"He's still here, though, right?" I asked, groping for a tissue, again out of habit. I was snot-free. "At the house? He didn't move out?"

"Not that I know of, honey. Probably just back to his old room while he sorts things out." I stared down at the table, and Jess smoothed my crumpled bangs out of my eyes. "Poor Bets. If it's not one thing it's another. You want me to stay in tonight?"

"Yeah, we could—no!"

"Oh, that's flattering," she grumbled.

"No, I mean . . . tonight's the big night. Your date with Nick. You can't miss it."

"I can reschedule," she said gently.

"My ass!"

"And that's one thing not on the date agenda," she said cheerfully. "He might have asked me out because he knows you're taken—"

"Am I?" I sulked.

"But one thing we're not going to do is talk about your ass. Nor your tits, nor your scintillating personality—which, I gotta tell you, ain't so great right now."

She was teasing and I smiled, a little. "No rescheduling. You're going. I'll—I'll find something to do."

On cue, the swinging doors on the east end of the kitchen whooshed open and Jon walked in like the world's youngest gunslinger. "Anybody up to telling me the story of their life?" he chirped, waving his Sidekick.

"Well," Jess told me, getting up from her seat, "if whatever you did was evil, and I'm not saying it was, because your word's good enough for me, but if it was, you're gonna be punished for it right about now."

CHAPTER 19

"Have you, uh, seen Sinclair around tonight?"

Jon snorted. "Not hardly. We sort of stay out of each other's way. I get the feeling he's not too crazy about me staying here."

"Well, it's not his house, now is it?" I asked sharply. Oh, great. Yell at the kid because your fiancé's not talking to you. "Sorry. I'm grumpy tonight."

"Because you haven't fed?" he asked eagerly, Sidekick poised. I saw he had flipped it around so he could tap on the tiny keyboard.

"No. But I'll worry about that some other night. Listen, Jon, if I do this for you, you've got to do something for me."

"I understand Betsy." He looked around; yes, we were alone

in the cavernous parlor. We'd moved there after the house-keeper got back from Rainbow and shooed us out. "I don't—uh—approve of that sort of—um—thing, but you're so—I mean, I'll make an exception for you." He bravely pulled off his T-shirt and inched closer to me. "Besides, it'll be good for the book."

"Ick! No!" I shoved him away, and he went flying over the end of the couch and crashed into the carpet. Dust flew. He coughed. I freaked. "Sorry, sorry, sorry!" I hurried around the couch and helped him up. "I didn't mean to shove you so hard."

"S'okay," he gasped, in the middle of a major coughing spasm. "M'sorry, too."

"It's my fault. I guess I was vague. No, I'm afraid the favor I've got in mind is a lot worse than sucking your blood."

"Whatever it is," he choked, "I'll do it. But first . . . you gotta get someone in here with a vacuum, I mean, right now."

"Who do you think you're talking to? Jon, I couldn't find the vacuum if you stuck a gun in my ear. Which if memory serves, you have."

He reddened and settled himself on a chair across from me. "That stuff's all over with, now."

"And we of the vampire community are grateful, believe me."

"We're talking about you," he said. "Why don't you start at the beginning?"

"Well, I was born in a small town in Minnesota, Cannon Falls, and I went to school at Cannon Falls Elementary, where

Mrs. Schultz was my favorite teacher. We moved to Burnsville when I was—"

"No," he interrupted, "I mean, the beginning, when you became a vampire."

"Oh. Kind of a short bio. I mean, not much has happened to me yet. As a vampire, I mean."

He rolled his eyes. "Betsy, I really like you and you're cute and all, but you are *so* full of crap."

"I am not! I haven't even been a vampire for a year, is what I meant, and I was a human for th—for twenty-five years at least. Hell, the Miss Burnsville pageant was way more stressful than vampire politics."

"Yeah, I'll get some of that stuff later for fill-in," he promised, but he was lying. "Let's get to the good stuff."

I sighed. "All right, all right. The good stuff. Well, I guess the good stuff starts on the last day. And it sucked, let me tell you. In fact, the day I died started out bad and got worse in a hurry . . ."

CHAPTER 20

"... and then you jumped off the roof of the mortuary and got run over by a garbage truck."

"Jon, there's no need to read it back to me; I know the story."

He laughed. "It's an incredible story! I'm reading it back to be sure I'm not fucking up anything. As it is, no one's going to think this is real."

"Well, good." We were in the entryway, and I was shrugging into my coat. Laura was here, coming up the walk, and she and I were baby-sitting Baby Jon tonight. "Because the whole point is, you're *pretending* it's a real bio about a vampire."

"I know, I know, you only told me a million times. Let's see ..."

"Jon, I gotta go. Can we pick this up tomorrow?"

"Yeah, let me just be sure I've got everything so far . . . you tried to drown yourself in the Mississippi River, you tried to electrocute yourself, tried to poison yourself with a bottle of bleach, and then stole a butcher knife and tried to stab yourself to death? Is that all?"

"Uh . . ." I wasn't about to go into the rapists I'd accidentally killed. "Pretty much."

Laura walked in—I'd told her weeks ago to stop with the knocking already—and said cheerfully, as she always did, "Good evening, darling sister. Ready to go?"

"Yeah." So, so ready. I wasn't up for another round of *This Is Your Life*. "Laura, have you met Jon? Jon, this is my sister, Laura."

She was having her usual effect on men, I could see: Jon had dropped his Sidekick. And hadn't noticed. Dust was probably cramming its delicate little circuits, and Jon hadn't noticed.

Instead, he was staring at my sister, and I couldn't blame him: she made Michelle Pfeiffer look like a hag. Tonight she was wearing moon boots (they were in, then out, and now in again, and I didn't care how often they came back in, I hated them, I wasn't a damn astronaut), black jeans, and a huge dark blue poofy parka that should have made her look like a blonde Michelin Man but, because God was cruel, did not.

"You never told me you had a sister," he said, looking deep into Laura's blue, blue eyes.

"You never told me you had a Jon." She giggled, obviously liking what she saw as well.

"I never told you I have a bleeding ulcer, either. Barf out, you guys. Come on, Laura, we'll be late."

"It was nice meeting you," she said, holding out a mittened hand.

"Meetcha, too," he mumbled, still gaping. He had goose bumps as big as cherries, but he didn't seem to notice he was standing shirtless in subzero cold.

"I hope to see you again soon."

"Blurble," he replied. At least that's what I think he said.

"Well, 'bye!" I said loudly—no mistaking *that,* I hoped. I practically pushed Laura out the front door and slammed it behind us.

"Oh, he was cute!" she was already gushing as we walked to the car. I trudged; she skipped. "Where do you know him from? Does he have a girlfriend? Of course he has a girlfriend."

"Laura, take a pill."

"Only if you stop being one," she snarked back. A mittened hand flew to her perfect, bow-shaped mouth. "Oh, I'm sorry! It's just . . . I'm a little nervous about tonight."

"Baby Jon won't bite. He doesn't have any teeth. He might puke on you, though."

"I've baby-sat before," she said happily. "It won't be the first time."

"Heck, I've been on dates that weren't so pleasant."

CHAPTER 21

The Ant greeted us with, "Get inside quick! There's a killer on the loose!" She grabbed me by the jacket collar—the first time she'd touched me in years—and hauled me into the foyer. Laura hurried in behind me just in time to avoid the door being slammed in her face.

"Those aren't killers," I explained, unbuttoning my coat. "They're Cub Scouts. They just want to sell you some wreaths and wrapping paper."

"Very funny, Betsy." The Ant was quite the wreath herself in a dress of poison green, which she had trimmed with a glittery red belt two inches wide, long fake red fingernails, and large red hoop earrings. Her lipstick matched her accessories, and her eyelids were as blue as the Caribbean. Her fake eyelashes were so long I at first thought a couple centipedes had crawled up there and died.

"No, it's the Driveway Killer," she was insisting, helping Laura (Laura had that effect on people) off with her big puffy coat. "He struck again! Took one of my neighbors right out of her driveway. At first we thought she'd, you know, just left—her husband—" The Ant made the universal "drinky drinky" motion with her thumb and forefinger. "But then her body turned up in the parking lot of the Lake Street Wal-Mart. Lake Street! Can you imagine? How tacky!"

"Er," was all Laura managed. The Ant could tax even her formidable powers of niceness.

"I'm sorry about your neighbor," I said, and I meant it, though the sentiment was probably wasted on the Ant, who apparently thought where your body turned up was far more important than how you lived your life.

"She was just minding her own business, coming in the house—or going, we're not sure which—and he *grabbed* her. I've been scared out of my wits ever since!"

"That's hard to imagine," I said sweetly.

"So you have to be very careful around here, girls."

I assumed she was talking to Laura.

"If something happened to you, I don't know what I'd do."

I was, against all my better instincts, touched. "Aw, Antonia. I don't know what to say."

"We'll be careful," Laura promised.

The baby monitor was on the little table for the car keys, and we could hear a thin wailing coming out from it. "Please,

please be careful! Nobody else will sit with Baby Jon while he's like this."

"Jesus, Antonia. He's got colic, not rabies."

"And I'm late."

"We got here right on time, so I don't want to hear anything out of you. When did he eat last?"

"The baby nurse left all that on a note on the fridge." The Ant was putting on her black wool coat. Her hair didn't move, which was a good trick considering it was shoulder length. "The party is supposed to be over around one."

"Where is Mr. Taylor?" Laura asked.

"Oh, he's . . ." The Ant made a vague gesture. "Don't worry, if I have too much to drink I'll get a cab."

"Thank goodness," I said. "If you get too blitzed, just take a nap in the driveway and wait around for company."

She glared. "I suppose you think you're being funny again."

I glared. "A little funny."

Laura walked in the direction of the kitchen.

The Ant left.

I went upstairs, scooped up my squalling brother, and snuggled him to my shoulder while he gasped and decided to knock off with the crying. My finely tuned vampire senses informed me he didn't need a diaper change.

We went back downstairs and caught up with Laura, who was standing at the main counter reading a careful, detailed note signed Jennifer Clapp, R.N.

"She has a baby nurse, and she needs us?" She clucked her tongue at Jon, who grunted in return.

"The nurse only works business hours. And my dad put his foot down about a night nurse when the Ant's home all day."

"Mr. Taylor said no to her?"

"It happens occasionally." Propping Jon's well-cushioned bottom on my forearm and his head on my shoulder, I opened the fridge and grimaced. It was full of skim milk, iceberg lettuce, soy sauce, Egg Beaters, and bottles of formula. If I was alive, that'd be a real problem. Poor Laura!

And "Mr. Taylor"? Laura's biological father. Nobody knew that little factoid but me, her, and the devil.

It was really complicated and would have even been silly if it wasn't so frightening. See, the devil possessed my stepmother for a while. And I think it's telling to report the Ant was (is!) such a miserable human being that *no one* noticed. I mean, how friggin' unbelievable is that? "Oh, you're evil and insane and running over pedestrians with your bicycle and granting evil wishes and encouraging people to jump off tall buildings . . . same old, same old, eh, Antonia?"

Anyway. So my dad's second wife was possessed by the devil for a while, yes, that's right, *the* devil, and had a baby, my sister Laura. And then went back to Hell.

The Ant, "coming to" with a drooly baby to take care of, promptly *dumped* Laura in the waiting room of a hospital and went back to her old life without looking back.

So—here's where it gets weird—the Ant and my dad are Laura's biological parents. And the devil is her mother. *And* Laura was adopted by the Goodmans (come on! The

Goodmans?), and raised in the suburbs of Minneapolis.

Have I mentioned her unholy hell-powers, like the bow made of hellfire and the way she can eat whatever she wants and never get a pimple?

So. It was a little weird when she referred to our—*her*—father as "Mr. Taylor." It was always "Mr. Taylor" or "Betsy's father." I had no idea how to handle it, so I just let it go. Just another thing hanging over my head like a wobbly guillotine.

"There isn't shit to eat," I announced, shutting the door, "as usual."

"We can have a pizza delivered." She held out her arms, and I handed the baby to her.

"*I* don't care; I can't eat it anyway. It's you I'm worried about. I get desperate enough, I can always drink the bottle of soy sauce. Mmmm . . . salty. Anyway, did you eat supper before you came over?"

"No," she admitted.

"God, how pathetic are we? Don't start," I warned the baby, who had stiffened in Laura's arms and looked ready to start with the yowling again. "I'm thirty and I'm baby-sitting and scrounging in the fridge for a meal. Next I'll be calling my boyfriend to tell him to come over so we can make out."

"At least you have a boyfriend," Laura pointed out.

I smiled sourly and said nothing.

"He's *sooooo* cute," Laura cooed. Tonight Baby Jon was wearing a T-shirt, Pampers, and thick green socks. He'd put on a little weight, but he still looked more like a hairless, angry rat than the plump Gerber babies I saw on TV. "Isn't he just the darlingest thing you've ever seen?"

"This is a scary side of you, Laura, and I thought I'd seen the really frightening stuff."

"Goooooooo," she replied, tickling Baby Jon under his pointy chin. Jon glared at her and then the odor of his discontent filled the air. "Oooooh, someone needs a diaper change." She looked at me.

"Daughter of the devil," I said.

"Vampire queen."

"Okay, okay, I'll do it. Gimme him."

Jon chuckled when I took him back, which, given his age, I knew was impossible. He wasn't really laughing, just like he wasn't really glaring. Still, it was cute.

I pretended he really liked me, though at this age he couldn't pick me out of a lineup. I cuddled him close all the way up the stairs, when Laura couldn't see.

The truth was, nights like this were the highlight of my life right now. I jumped whenever the Ant called. Bottom line? Baby Jon was the closest I was ever going to get to having a baby of my own. No tears, no sweat, no periods . . . no babies.

Ever.

Sinclair and I could do a lot—would do a lot, if he ever got over our little problem of the month. But we couldn't make our own babies.

Jess told me over and over not to be silly, there were only a zillion babies in the world who needed good homes, and

Marc backed her up with horror stories of abuse from the E.R. She was right—they were both right—and I tried not to feel bad.

But at thirty, I hadn't thought I was forever turning my back on having my own babies. It was funny . . . I'd never seriously thought about having a baby. I just always assumed I would. And then I died. Isn't that the way it goes sometimes?

"It's dumb," I told Baby Jon, stripping him of the nasty diaper and setting it aside (I would later place it beneath the Ant's bed, where she'd go crazy trying to find it). "Dead people can't do lots of things. Walk, talk, have sex. Get married. Bitch. I'm lucky I can do anything, instead of just hanging out in a coffin and slowly turning into fertilizer. So what do I focus on? The good stuff? The cool powers? No, I piss and moan because Sinclair can't knock me up. Does that make sense? Does that sound like a person who's counting her blessings?"

"Fleh," Jon replied.

"Tell me." I sprinkled him like salt on a roast, rubbed in the powder, and then put a new diaper on him. He sighed and waved his little arms, and I caught a tiny hand and kissed it. He promptly scratched me with his wolverine-like nails, but I didn't mind.

CHAPTER 22

"I can't thank you enough for coming out," the Ant said. Again. To Laura.

"It was our pleasure, Mrs. Taylor. Your son is adorable."

The Ant looked doubtfully at the monitor, which occasionally vibrated with Baby Jon's snores. "It's . . . it's nice of you to say so. I hope he wasn't any trouble."

"He's *dar*ling!" Laura exclaimed, brushing spit-up off her shoulder.

"Yeah, a laugh a minute," I grumped. "And I'm busy tomorrow, so don't even think about it."

"I'm free," Laura piped up.

"That's all right, girls. My fund-raiser was postponed, anyway. And Freddy can come over then, anyway."

"Freddy?" I asked sharply. "Hooked-on-her-migraine-medication Freddy?"

"She's not hooked," the Ant, no stranger to substance abuse, insisted. "She just has a lot of migraines."

"I don't care if she has a lot of brain tumors! She's not watching Baby Jon!"

"It's not up to you," the Ant snapped. Then, "Who?"

"When is your meeting?" Laura interjected quickly. "I'm sure we can work something out."

The Ant puffed a strand of hair out of her face, which didn't move. "Laura, I appreciate that *you* are trying to do *your* best, but there's nothing to work out. I'll be the one to decide what's best for the baby."

I got ready to pull her head off her shoulders and kick it up the stairs, a grisly surprise for my dad if he ever got back, when Laura asked, "Like you decided before?"

Whoa.

"What?" the Ant asked.

"What?" I warned, frozen in the act of reaching for the Ant's tiny head.

"The baby. From before. You decided what was best for her . . . that you couldn't take care of her."

"Now?" I asked my sister, who had apparently gone insane when I wasn't looking. "You're picking now to do this?" Rotten timing: a genetic legacy poor Laura couldn't escape.

"I don't—I don't—"

I dropped my arms to my sides. The Ant had a whole lot more to worry about right now than beheading by stepdaughter.

"It was a good choice," Laura added, "if it was the one that was best for you. Still, do you ever wonder what happened to her? Do you ever think about her?"

"No," the Ant said, looking right into Laura's incredible blue eyes. "I never think of her. Just like when you aren't here, I never think of you. That was a long time ago, and I never think about how when you wear your hair pulled up, you look like my mother. The way she looked when she liked us more than the bottle. I never think about that, and I never think about her, and I never, ever, ever think about you."

"Oh," Laura gulped, as I fought not to fall into the hall plant. She knew! She knew! And she never said anything! "I see."

"You're a real nice girl, Laura. I was happy to meet you. I'm always happy when you can come by. But it's late, and it's time for you to get out of here."

"Of—of course."

"A heart-stopping pleasure," I said, following Laura out the door. "Just like always. You jackass."

The Ant didn't say anything. Just stood in the doorway for a long time. Making sure the Driveway Killer didn't get us. Or making sure we really left.

CHAPTER 23

We walked to my car. We got in. I started it up. We sat for a minute, waiting for the heater to kick in. (We weren't too worried about the Driveway Killer.) We pulled out. We watched the Ant shut her front door. (She must have frozen her treadmilled ass right off, watching us leave.)

I couldn't stand it half a second longer and blurted, "I can't believe she knew. I can't believe she knew! She probably knew the minute she laid eyes on you, since you apparently look like her dead alcoholic mother. And she just . . . just let us come over and baby-sit! All those times! And you were at the baby shower! You brought her a fucking present from Tiffany's!"

"She is . . . a strong woman," Laura said faintly.

"She is a *YAAAAAAAAAAAAAGGGGGGGGGGG- GGHH-HHHHHH*!"

"What? What?" Laura was twisting around in her seat, her hand on an invisible sword hilt. There was a sword there, but it only came out when Laura wanted it. And only she could touch it.

I looked at Laura, looked back up at my rearview mirror at the sallow blonde who was sitting in my backseat, and looked back at Laura. "Yuh—uh—I saw a squirrel."

Laura was looking straight into the backseat, on the floor, around the car. "For goodness's sake, where? Behind your brake?"

The blonde stared at me, and I tried to pull my attention back to France Avenue. "It just . . . scared the hell out of me. Popping up like that." I glared into the mirror. "Without warning."

"Sorry," the blonde said.

"Well, don't scare me like that!" Laura snapped. "It's been a stressful enough evening."

"Tell me about it," the blonde in the back said.

My heart was galloping along from the adrenaline rush (okay, adrenaline tickle, and "galloping" meant about ten beats a minute), which was stressful enough without having to watch Laura, the ghost in the back, and the road.

"Were you—did you—" I finally spit it out. "Were you planning this? Scratch that: how long have you been planning it?"

"I didn't really plan it," she confessed. "I *carpe'd* the *diem*."

"Well, Laura, I hope you—hope you know that for the—for your mother, that was pretty good. I mean, she was almost nice. Which for her, was *really* nice."

"Yes, I know."

"Just give her time. She'll, uh . . ." *Grow a soul?* "And Laura . . . don't take this the wrong way or anything, but if you were planning on saying anything to our father . . ."

"Christ," the woman in the back said. "This is better than *Days of Our Lives*."

"Shut up!"

"That's good advice," Laura said.

"No, uh . . . I mean, I wouldn't recommend . . . maybe not right now, anyway . . ."

"Don't worry," Laura said, tight-lipped. "I wasn't."

"That's a load off my mind," the dead woman in the back said.

CHAPTER 24

"Well, it's been"—*Upsetting. Tense. If I was alive, I'd have shit myself at least twice in the last hour*—"really something."

"You're not going in?" Laura asked, pausing outside the front door. None of us used any of the side doors. I didn't know why. Yes I did. Nobody wanted to get mistaken for a servant. Even the servants (the housekeepers, the plant lady, the gardener) used the front door.

"No, no. I'm going to stay out here"—in the freezing, subzero temperature and bitter wind—"and get some fresh air." Even though I didn't breathe.

Laura's perfect forehead wrinkled. "Are you sure?"

"What," the ghost protested, "you're not going to let me in?"

"No, it's a real nice night. And I want to . . . look at the garden in the moonlight."

"You've got to be shitting me," the ghost protested. "I've been stuck outside for more than a week, and you're not letting me come in?"

"On second thought," I said, "I will come in."

"Let's hope you're a better hostess than driver," the dead woman bitched.

"You shut up. You're getting your way aren't you?"

"All I said was 'are you sure,'" Laura protested.

"Sorry, sorry. I'm pissed at the Ant on your behalf, and it's coming out at totally inappropriate times."

"That cow," the ghost said. "She let her little yappy dog poop in my yard every damn week. She thought I wasn't looking."

"Enough," I said.

"I agree," Laura almost snapped. "It's been a long night."

"Honey, you don't know what the hell you're talking about."

"Are you still planning on meeting up tomorrow?"

"Christmas shopping," Laura agreed, calming down before my eyes. At least her hair hadn't changed color, thank goodness. "I'll meet you here at six, all right?"

"I can't friggin' wait," the dead woman said.

"All right," I said. "Good night."

I watched Laura drive off in her smiley-face yellow VW, which her too-good-to-be-true-but-they-really-were-good adoptive parents had saved up for three years to buy her.

I looked at the ghost, who was a couple inches shorter than me, with dark blond hair pulled back in a short ponytail. She was wearing a faded green Sea World sweatshirt with the sleeves pushed up to her elbows and black stretch pants. Socks. No shoes or coat. But of course, she wasn't cold.

"Why don't you come in?"

"Why don't I?" she agreed. "Thanks for the ride. I thought I was going to be stuck in Edina forever. Talk about hell."

She walked through me into the house, which felt exactly like someone throwing a bucket of ice water in my face. "Dammit!" I gasped, lunging to shut the door.

"Sorry," she said smugly.

CHAPTER 25

"You're back!" Jon cried.

"Jeez, let me get my coat off. And not now, okay?"

"Who's the hottie?" the ghost said, ogling. She passed her hand through his crotch, which, thankfully, he didn't notice.

"Stop that! It's against the law to do that even if you are dead."

"What?" Jon asked.

"I'm getting my thrills wherever I can," the ghost explained, "so off my case."

Tina had followed Jon into the entryway. "Good evening, Your Majesty. I was just on my way out."

"How many weirdos live in this place?" the ghost asked. "It's like *The Real World with Losers.*"

"All those shows are like that," I told her. To Jon: "Seriously, not now. I've got some other errands and stuff to do before the sun comes up."

"Oh, don't mind me," the ghost sniffed. "I'm sure you'd much rather be getting naked with Super Hottie."

"I don't want to get naked with him, for the millionth time!"

I didn't realize it, but judging from the echoes in the entryway, I had screamed it.

"Whoa," Jon said, backing off.

"Excuse my boldness, Majesty, but do you have . . . a guest?"

"Dah-DAH-DAHHHHHHH," the ghost hummed dramatically.

I put a hand over my eyes. "God, yes. And she's really annoying."

"Why don't you drop dead?" the ghost suggested.

"Too late," I snapped back. "See her, Tina? About this high . . ." I held my hand up to my nose. "Blond hair in a tacky ponytail, tacky sweatshirt, no shoes."

"If I'd known I'd have to walk around in sweat socks for eternity," the ghost protested, "I'd have dressed up a little."

"Ah, yes," Tina said, squinting and then brightening as the ghost slowly became visible to her. "Good evening, miss. My name is Tina; this is Elizabeth, The One."

"Wait a minute. I go days and days and no one can see me, and now she says so and you can, too?"

"She is my queen," Tina said simply.

"The way it works is, I'm a vampire—"

"Get out!" the ghost gasped.

"I swear!"

"I just thought you were a freak, like that kid in the movie. I didn't know you were, like, dead already."

"Well, I am, so let's not rub it in, okay?"

"Oh, I have to be sensitive to your feelings about being dead?"

"That's not what I meant," I said through gritted teeth. "And if you'll shut up a minute, I'll explain how Tina can see you. Not only am I a vampire, I'm sort of the boss of all of them. And one of the (dumb) rules is, if I see a ghost and tell a vampire to see the ghost, they can see the ghost."

"How totally lame," she commented. "It sounds made up to me."

"Well, it isn't," I snapped. "And you should be a lot nicer, in my opinion."

"Well, nobody *asked* for your opinion, honey. It's nice to meet you," she told Tina. "Can you help me?"

"*I'm* supposed to help you."

The ghost looked at me doubtfully. "Yeah, well, great. Looks like I've got all the help I need."

"Why don't we have a seat in the parlor?" Tina suggested.

"Yeah," I agreed. "Why don't we? It's the first room on your right." As we followed the ghost, I practically whispered to Tina, "Have you, uh, seen Sinclair tonight?"

"No," she murmured back. "I haven't seen him in two days. I did not wish to pry, but . . ."

"Ooooooh!" the ghost said loudly, phasing through the parlor wall. "More dramatic shenanigans."

I sighed and followed her. I took the door, though.

"First things first," the ghost said. She didn't sit down, but we did, so we were sort of staring up at her, craning our necks. "I'm dead, right? I mean, I'm pretty sure. But I just wanted to double-check."

"Yes," Tina said.

"We're sorry," I added. "For what it's worth, you were way too young. You look about my age."

"Don't flatter yourself; I'm only twenty-six. I mean, I was twenty-six." She sighed and looked through us. Literally. "I figured. The last thing I remember is this huge crash, this big light in my brain, and then all of a sudden I'm back in my neighborhood and nobody can see me. That damn dog of Antonia's pooped *through* me."

"How can we help you?" Tina asked, all business.

"Sorry about your dying," I added.

"I'll tell you how I can help," she said. "My name is Cathie Robinson, and I'm—"

"The latest victim of the Driveway Killer," Tina said. She looked at me. "The *Trib* ran a story when her—ah—when your body was found, Mrs. Robinson."

"In a parking lot, right?" she asked glumly. She sat down, phased through the couch, and disappeared into the floor. We heard a muffled "Shit!" and then she struggled back up into the parlor. "In a fucking parking lot!"

"Yes, I'm afraid so."

"Sorry," I said again, because honestly, I couldn't think of a thing to say.

"That piece of shit! That little *lowlife*!"

"Do you remember anything about . . . dying?" Tina asked tactfully . . . as tactfully as such a thing could be asked, anyway. "About where you were taken? About the killer?"

"Honey?" Cathie asked, fixing Tina with a sudden, piercing gaze. "I remember *everything*."

Tina smiled. It was awful; you could practically see her drooling at the thought of getting her fangs into the Driveway Killer. "Then at last, you're having some luck, Mrs. Robinson. A friend of ours is on the task force."

Cathie sighed and leaned back (carefully, so she wouldn't fall through the wall). "I knew there was a reason I was following you around," she told me.

"Tell us everything. We'll worry about the difficulties later."

"What difficulties? I'll tell you where he is—where he took me, anyway—and you go get him!"

"Our friend—the one on the task force—not only doesn't know we're vampires, he certainly doesn't know we can speak with the dead. Sharing this information with him without compromising our safety will be difficult."

"But we'll figure out a way," I hastily advised Cathie, who was starting to look superpissed. "Obviously, catching this guy is *primo numero uno* on our list."

"Well, I should fucking well hope so!" she snapped. "I left

a family, you know. And I was a good girl—I should be in heaven right this minute. The only reason I'm still here is to help you catch that scumshit, that piece of shit jerkoff, that assface."

I was still admiring Cathie's rich and colorful vocabulary when I heard a familiar step in the hall.

"Tell Tina the whole story," I said hurriedly, leaping to my feet.

"Hey!" Cathie protested. "Where the hell do you think you're going?"

"It's much more important to tell Tina than me," I said, practically running to catch up to him. "She's, like, ten times smarter than me anyway."

"*That* I figured out on my own. But what's more important than this?"

Dead people, I thought, darting into the entryway. *They're the most selfish people on the planet.*

"Sinclair!" I hollered. "Wait up!"

CHAPTER 26

"Where—where are you going?"

"Out," he replied.

That much was obvious; he was wearing his black wool greatcoat and his Kenneth Cole shoes, which were shined to a high gloss. He was tapping his black leather gloves impatiently into his palm while he politely waited for me to Get On With It.

"Out—how come?"

"I need to feed, Elizabeth," he said simply.

I almost reeled at the implications of that. Since we'd been together, we sort of had an unwritten rule about feeding . . . we only did each other.

That was the trouble with unwritten rules. Anybody could rewrite them . . . or ignore them.

"But . . . don't you want to . . . with me?" I couldn't believe I was asking this; me, the one who was totally squicked out by blood-sharing. But the thought of him finding some pretty girl . . . dazzling her . . . taking from her . . . and she'd fall in love with him of course . . . and then what would he do? Keep her?

It wasn't like he hadn't done it before. Hell, he used to have a harem of girls who *looooooooved* it when he drank from them. He gave them all tons of money and sent them on their way when he moved in, and that was that. Nice and neat.

Except now . . .

His glove-tapping sped up. "I had assumed, after what happened earlier, that such things were off limits. To both of us."

"Well, when you *ASSuME,* you make an *ass* out of *you* and *me*. So there!"

"What?"

"We just had a fight, that's all, just a stupid fight. It's not the end of everything. And frankly, I don't want you going out in the cold and biting some other woman, so there!"

"Another 'so there.' You must feel quite strongly about the situation."

"Well, you freaked out when Jon, who I have no intention of biting or boning, moved in. Now you're off to the races, and you're all surprised that I have a problem with it?"

His mouth tightened; it look more like a scar than lips I had come to know well. "That is hardly the same thing."

"Wrong, suck-o! It's exactly the same thing."

"Very well." In a flash—I could see what happened only if I replayed it in my head—he dropped his gloves, kicked out of his shoes, and dragged me up the stairs. In the time it took me to realize he had dropped his gloves, he had kicked my (our) bedroom door shut, jerked my head to one side, and sank his fangs into me.

I screamed, shocked to my toes at what he had done—no, *how* he had done it. I tried to get free, but he had one hand across my shoulders and the other hand was forcing my chin to the side, giving him easy access to my jugular. Wriggling free was like trying to get free of a tree that had planted itself around me.

"Stop it, Eric, stop it, please stop it," I begged, and hated myself for begging.

Yes stop what are you doing why are you hurting her you'll have your pride and that's all you'll have so stop it stop it STOP IT!

He pulled back and licked my blood off his teeth. He watched the small trickle of blood travel down my neck, caught it with a finger, and licked that dry, too. Then he let go of me and I spun away.

I knew it was coming. He knew it was coming. And he stood still for it. Penance? I didn't give a fuck. I slapped him so hard he staggered back, bounced off the wall, and lay on the floor like a stunned cockroach.

I stood over him, saw his fangs were still out, and slapped a hand over the bite on my neck.

"I said I was sorry, okay?" I hated the way my voice shook. Why hadn't I seen that coming? Just how dumb was I? "I said it. And I'm done saying it. So you're either gonna get over it, or you won't. Once you decide *that,* move in here or don't. And I mean *move in,* none of this showing up at night for blood and sex and then leaving. But enough of this sulking and pissing and moaning, okay? Believe it or not, I've got bigger problems than your bruised ego. Now get the fuck out. Here, I'll help you."

I bent down, meaning to pick him up and throw him out the window—I was pretty sure I was strong enough to do it, and was dying to find out. I had also counted on Eric's weird contrite mood, which didn't last very long, as I found out when he yanked me down on top of him.

"I guess you didn't hear my speech," I said through gritted teeth. "I guess I gotta go through the whole thing again."

"I heard it. What are your bigger problems?"

"What is this, a quiz show? *Undead Wheel of Fortune?*"

"You said 'believe it or not, I've got bigger problems than your bruised ego.'" His eyes were about two inches from my own. I could smell my blood. I hated myself for wanting him to take another bite. "I was wondering what they were."

"After the stunt you just pulled? I'm not telling you a fucking thing, pal!"

"Because I am a king who does not 'noe' the queen's ways," he said quietly.

"No, jackass, because you just came up here and practically *raped* me because you're in a bad mood! I don't give a shit that you can't read my mind when we're boning, and frankly, you should be relieved! Do you really want all that stuff in your head?"

"It's only a matter of time," he said in a monotone that scared me to death. "If you wish, you may throw me out the window now."

"Sinclair!" I slapped him across the face, a sort of "wake up, you're on fire!" smack, but he didn't say anything. "Dude, you have got to pull yourself together!" *I really need you now. More than I ever did, so please, please get it together, I'm sorry, you're sorry, everybody's sorry, can we please be the way we were a week ago?*

"On the contrary, I have finally seen things for exactly what they are. It's . . . distressing."

"Eric, come on. It's been a rotten day, and you already scared the shit out of me once."

"Oh, that," he said absently. "I apologize. I was hungry, and you were annoying. It won't happen again."

Don't say that! It wasn't what you did, it was how you did it, please don't say that!

"I'll go," he said quietly, "but before I do, I'd like to remind you that it's very likely you could have a living baby with a living man. I know how fond you are of Baby Jon, and I'm certain you could have one of your own once you come to your senses and jettison me from your life."

"But—I could? But—but I don't want—"

Oblivious to my massive confusion, he sat up and gently picked me up off him, the way you shoo a ladybug off your hand when you're going inside, stood, placed me on the bed, turned, and left.

CHAPTER 27

"Hey, wake up."

I burrowed farther under the covers, a big undead worm.

"Hey, Betsy. Wake up."

"Hnnnnnnwwwww," I mumbled, which any sane person would translate as "Go away, I'm sleeping."

"Your sister is beating the living shit out of that vampire who lives in the basement."

That got my attention. I sat up and there was Cathie, shoeless and looking scared, sitting in Marie's Chair. "What? What are you talking about?"

"Your sister. She came over early, I guess for Christmas shopping? She went downstairs, and I was bored out of my tits, so I followed her. She started beating up that long-haired guy in the basement, the one who can't talk. I didn't want to ask your friends to step in—one of your roommates looks like she's on a date, and her date is actually here, wandering around waiting for her—"

"Christ," I groaned.

"—and you're the only vampire I could wake up."

I tossed the blankets back and glanced at the clock: 5:35 P.M. I'd slept late, but the others wouldn't be awake for a few minutes yet, not until the sun fell down.

"Nice pajamas. Did you get them at a garage sale?"

I started for the stairs at a dead run. I was out my door in half a second, on the stairs in another second, and pounding down the basement steps while the blanket was still falling to the floor upstairs.

I screeched to a halt in front of the long, bare area of the basement we called the sparring section.

Cathie had not been exaggerating. Laura *was* fighting George, and if he hadn't been dead before, he would be soon. It's not that she was such a good fighter—though she was—it's that he wasn't fighting back. Every blow she landed sounded sickening and looked worse.

"Laura!"

"Fight, you demon spawn, *fight*!"

"Laura, stop it!"

"You *fight* so I can send you to my mother. You *fight* so you can tell her I'm doing *just fine* up here and she need not interfere . . . *again*!"

Laura's hair, I was dismayed to see, was flame red—

the color of sullen coals after a raging fire. Her eyes were the color of fall grass—green, but dying. Gone was the rosy-cheeked blond teen we all knew and liked. We were here with the devil's daughter now.

"Jesus," Cathie murmured, finally making it back down to the basement.

"I wish," I said.

"What's wrong with her?"

"She has parental issues."

"No, *I've* got parental issues. She is fucked up severe."

"Later. *Laura!*" I bawled. "Get off him right now! *Now* now, not in a minute now!"

"Stay out of this, Betsy!" she shrilled back. She smacked George another good one—I could only imagine how much it must have hurt her hand, judging from how it split open George's cheek—and he reeled and almost went down, but didn't fight back.

"Laura, I hate to pull rank on you, but I'm the queen, and that's a subject so get your *fucking hands off him right now!*"

She smacked him again—wham*thud!*—I couldn't *believe* it. Was I even in the goddamned room?

I raced around them just as her sword materialized on her hip. I couldn't look at the thing—it was made of hellfire and gave me an instant headache, it was like looking into the sun—so I averted my gaze and somehow—I'm still not quite sure how I pulled this off—somehow I was in front of George, my arms spread out protectively, and that's how my sister accidentally plunged her blade into my chest.

CHAPTER 28

"Betsy? Betsy? Betsy?"

"Gllllkkkkkkkkkk!"

Is that me? No. Who's choking? It's not me, right?

"Laura, I am quite fond of you—" Sinclair? What was he doing down here? And it sounded like he was throttling my sister . . . I had no idea how I felt about that, to be honest. Yay? Boo?

"Gggggllllkkkkk!"

"—yes, thank you, but if she dies, I'm afraid you will die as well. It's this odd little territorial tic I have. I realize it's a problem, and I'm dealing with it, but right now I must stand by what I said."

"Betsy? Can you hear me?" Marc! That was Marc.

Excellent! Finally, he has a day off when it actually helps me.

"She's got a big fucking sword sticking out from between her boobs." That was Cathie. "Of course she can't hear you. Why am I even bothering to talk to you idiots?"

I'm not dead!

"I suppose it's no good looking for vital signs." Tina.

"Well, she doesn't have a pulse, and she's not breathing, so I'd say she's dead. Also, there's a big-ass sword sticking out of her chest."

"Duh!" Cathie shouted.

"But she's been dead before, so this is kind of a stumper for me."

Tina hmmmmed and then said, "For us as well . . . where's Nick?"

"Jessica's keeping him busy upstairs, thank God. Of all the stupid times for her to start dating again."

"Amen to that," I said and opened my eyes. I was startled to see Marc and Cathie had been right—there *was* a big-ass sword sticking out of my chest. I'd seen Laura stab vampires with it before, and they instantly disintegrated. I was sort of amazed to see I wasn't a pile of ashes. "Sinclair! Put her down. Laura, get over here. Get this thing out of me."

They both looked over at me, Laura's face so red it looked like she was going to pop a blood vessel. Which, given the firm grip Sinclair had on her throat, was probably imminent. He let go, and she hit the cement, gasping.

"I can't leave any of you people alone for one day without all hell breaking loose," I griped. "Where's George?"

"We put him in the shower to wash away the blood," Tina reported matter-of-factly. She was on one knee beside me and kept squeezing my arm as if to reassure herself that I wasn't going to disintegrate.

Laura had heaved herself to her knees and then her feet. If I were her, I wouldn't be so quick to turn my back on Sinclair, but she only had eyes for me as she staggered toward us.

"Betsy, oh Besty! Forgive me!" She tripped and fell but probably was going to get back on her knees anyway, judging from what came out next, which was: "I swear, you were not my target! I'm an unworthy treacherous bitch, one you have taken into your family, and I repaid you with—" She gestured at her sword. "Please, please, I beg your forgiveness. I—"

"Laura."

"Yes?"

"Can we do this after you've pulled this thing out of me?"

"Oh. Oh! Yes, of course. I—ah—no one's ever—" She grabbed the hilt with easy familiarity. "Either my sword passes harmlessly through them—it only disrupts magic—or it kills them. It's never . . . gotten stuck halfway."

I felt a little ill. "Well, can we get it un-stuck, please?"

"Yes, of course, but after causing you so much pain, I feel I must warn you it may hurt a bit—"

"Elizabeth!" Sinclair said sharply from his brooding corner. We all snapped around to gape at him; it was not a good thing when he raised his voice. "I must insist you cancel the wedding at once."

I gasped with fresh outrage. "And the hits just keep on coming! Cancel the weddi*arrrrrrrrgggggggg*!" I clutched my chest, which was hole-free, thank goodness. "That *did* hurt, you cow!"

"Perhaps less," he said, looking vastly relieved, "as you were distracted."

"Yeah, thanks for 'helping' me by scaring the shit out of me," I grumped as Tina and Marc helped me to my feet. Marc felt between my boobs, which I didn't take personally, and then circled around to feel my back.

"How do you feel?" Tina asked anxiously.

"Pissed off! I've been up for, what, ten minutes? Cripes. This is worse than prom '91. Laura, you've got some big-time explaining to do."

"Close your eyes," Marc told me, "and think of England." Then he pushed my pajama top up.

"Ack! It's chilly in here, stop that." I jerked away from him. "I'm pretty sure if I had a big old stab wound in my chest, we'd all know it."

"I can't believe you aren't dead!" Laura exclaimed. "I mean, I'm happy and everything, but I've never seen that happen before." Sinclair came up to our little group, and she sort of shrank away from him. "I tried to tell you . . . before . . . I didn't mean to stab her. She got between us."

"Yesssssssssss," Sinclair purred. "And who *were* you trying to stab when she, ah, got between you?"

"It wasn't . . . it wasn't for real." Laura suddenly looked about twelve years old. The braids helped. So did the fact that she'd put her sword away . . . to wherever it went when she wasn't killing vampires with it. "We were just practicing."

"I guess what happened at the Ant's bugged you more than you let on," I suggested.

Laura shrugged. She wouldn't look at any of us. Her hair was blond again, and her eyes were blue. The blue of the Ant's mother, apparently, or the devil.

"He's a feral vampire," she pointed out defensively. "It's not like I could have really hurt him . . . done some lasting damage."

Lie.

"It was just a training exercise."

Lie.

"It has nothing to do with my family life," she insisted, the third and (hopefully) final lie.

"It—"

You fight so I can send you to my mother!

"—doesn't—"

You fight so you can tell her I'm doing just fine up here!

"—mean anything."

"Oh, boy," Cathie said. Tina glanced over at her, but nobody else had a clue. "Did you say she had some parental issues? Because that's a pretty fucking big issue right there. I mean, come on, Liz. You don't believe this happy crappy, do you?"

"Don't call me that. It's all right, Laura," I said after an awkward moment. My life: a series of awkward moments. "It was an accident. I know you'd never want to hurt me."

"Yes, that's just right," she said, guileless blue eyes swimming with tears. "I'd never ever want to hurt you. I'd die before hurting you."

"Really?" Sinclair asked, head cocked to one side.

"Let me, ah, just go check on George, and we can go finish our shopping."

Her face lit up. "You—you still want to?"

"Are you kidding? What part of 'thirty percent off everything in the store' do you not get? It would take a lot more than this to keep me away. I'll meet you out at the car."

"Oh," she said sadly. "I guess this is the part where you all talk about what to do about me."

"It's more like a Secret Santa thing," I said, pushing her toward the stairs.

CHAPTER 29

"Jesus," I said, staring into the shower. "She kicked the living crap out of him."

"Yes."

"I don't suppose he said anything."

"No," Tina and Sinclair said in unison. Marc had gone back upstairs to take Jess aside and assure her all was well. Who knew what Nick was up to—hopefully not prying too much. Cathie, miffed we had let my sister "get away," had walked through a wall and went who-knew-where.

"Poor guy, minding his own business and she comes down here and starts whaling away on him."

I started to chew on my wrist—the usual quick pick-me-up for George—when Sinclair stopped me. "A large part of your sister's faith hinges on redemption. She does seem to feel badly about her part in this. So why not have *her* feed George for a day or two?"

"Oh, but that's pretty . . ." Diabolically mean. "Brilliant," I confessed. "Okay, I'll tell her that. She'll have to feed him, one way or another, until he's healed up from everything she did to him."

"And I—ah—must be sure that the—ah—" Tina was stammering like a blonde learning Latin. And I ought to know.

"Tina, what in the world is your problem?"

"The thing!" she blurted. "I must be sure the thing is also taken care of."

"What?" I asked, but Tina was already out of the shower room.

Leaving me with Sinclair, who wouldn't talk to me, and George, who couldn't.

Oh.

"Well." Cough, cough. "I guess I'd better get to shopping—"

"You seem to always be shot or stabbed or otherwise fatally attacked when I'm not around." And was that a smile, lurking in the corners of his mouth?

"Hey, I didn't do anything. I was minding my own business, and Laura stabbed me in the heart." Okay, even I knew how lame that sounded.

He *was* smiling. "Your sister will have some bruising."

"Okay. I'll break out the ice packs. For the record, I disapprove of the whole strangling thing."

The smile was gone, banished to wherever Sinclair's smiles go. "She is *extremely* lucky that's all she will have."

"Now, come on. It was an accident. You saw how upset she was after."

"She certainly *seemed* to be upset," he agreed.

"What? She was lying?"

"I don't know. That's part of what I don't like."

"Well, you shouldn't have picked her up like that and choked her like a rat, that's all I'm saying. Although it was kind of—never mind. Bad, bad Sinclair! But thanks for coming to the rescue. Again."

He sighed and brought me close to him; warily, I went. "No matter how angry I am with you, I cannot bear to see you hurt, or in trouble, it seems."

I felt like jumping up and down. I squashed the impulse. "That's because we're in *luurrrrrrrrvvvv.*"

He grimaced. "How enchanting."

"Listen, I've been thinking."

"How charming!"

"Shut your face. I really have. Been thinking, I mean. About the fight, and the things you said. Maybe we shouldn't get married," I said uneasily. The training of a lifetime of reading *Modern Bride* rose within me and screamed in horror, but dammit, this was bigger than what I wanted.

"Are you sure she didn't hit you on the head with that hellish thing?" he asked, feeling my forehead.

I slapped his hand away. "I'm serious. This sort of thing is always going to be happening to us. To our friends. There's always going to be some disaster that will threaten to ruin everything. You have to admit, this was minor, as far as this stuff goes. And worse is around the corner, guaranteed. Maybe . . ."

"No."

"I'm just saying . . ."

"You've said it yourself: you won't feel like you belong to me without this silly human ritual. So we are doing it, damn it all. And I am not going through a tasting menu again, or a flower meeting. No. Absolutely not."

"That's . . . so sweet," I said finally. "So you feel like you're not worthy of me, but you're insisting on a wedding, when before you implied that me changing the date means I secretly don't want to marry you. Is that about right?"

"Secretly or not, this human ritual obviously holds deep meaning for you. So we will do it. Then even you will admit you belong to me."

"Uh . . . we're not using 'obey' in the vows."

He smiled. "Aren't you in for a surprise, darling."

CHAPTER 30

"What just happened?" I asked Jon on the way to the front door. "Did we make up? Are we back together again? We were ever not together? Did he change his mind after he saw me get stabbed? Should I hold a grudge because of the whole felony assault thing in my bedroom? Or should we call it even because I smacked the shit out of him right after? And why am I asking you this stuff? Where's Tina? Where's Jess?"

"So it's true!" Jon cried, fumbling for his Sidekick with one hand and frantically brushing his shaggy bangs out of his eyes with the other. "Betsy, we've got to pick up where we left off."

"Shhhhhh!" I could hear Jess and Nick chit-chatting from the next room. "Not while Nick is here."

"Nick would be . . ." He consulted his tiny notes. "Detective Nick Berry. Ooh, yuck, that's inconvenient."

"To say the least. We're not sure what he knows, so for Christ's sake don't be babbling about vampires and swords and shit while he's around."

"Don't worry. You can count on me. You know you can."

"Well, thanks." I smiled at him. Then I frowned. "You know, I *was* excited about Jessica dating this guy, but now I'm starting to wonder . . ."

"But when can we get together again?" he whined.

"Come shopping with Laura and me. She knows most of my dirty little secrets. You wouldn't have to keep your mouth shut around her." And I had a feeling that what happened in the basement was going to be off-limits, conversation-wise, for a long, long time.

"Okay!" he said, and actually pumped his fist in the air. I cried dry tears over what a geek loser he was and went to get my coat.

Dear Betsy,
I died about ten years ago, and as you know, basi-
cally all I've cared about since is the thirst. But
things are different now. I've been keeping up with
my hometown newspaper, and I've read that my dad
is going to retire. He was only 39 when I became a
vampire. He's never seen me since, and neither has
anyone else in my family. What should I do? I know
I'm supposed to keep a low profile, but I really miss

*my folks and would like to see what they've been up
to.*

   Sign me,
   Family Friendly in Fridley

Dear Fridley,
*For crying out loud, go see your dad. If you don't
want them to know you're a vampire, make shit
up . . . you've been recruited by a secret government
agency and that's why you went missing for so long.
So secret you can't talk about it, or even stay very
long, but they should be superproud of you because
you're out saving the world.*

   *Something like that. Trust me, they'll be thrilled
you're not dead. They won't even think of awkward
questions until you're long gone.*

   Your queen,
   Betsy

CHAPTER 31

We had rolled past the third group of carolers when Jon made the comment, "This time of year must be hell on vampires. Literally hell."

I giggled. "Some carolers came to the house, and Tina and Sinclair ran down to the basement with their hands over their ears. And they don't go shopping with me, needless to say. A simple 'Merry Christmas' from a stranger gives them indigestion for the rest of the day."

At last, Laura laughed. She'd been driving like a robot: no speaking, no engaging, just stiff turns and shifts.

"But it doesn't bother you."

"Heck, no, I love this time of year."

"You're crazy to go to the mall the week before Christmas," Jon observed.

"Oh, shut up. What do you know about it?"

"I know I finished my Christmas shopping in October."

I shuddered. One of *those* freaks. More unnatural than the vampires, if you asked me.

"Is George going to be all right?" Laura asked timidly.

"Ah, George. Yes, let's get to it, shall we? Sinclair came up with a super punishment for you."

"Asshole," Jon muttered, almost too quietly for me to catch.

I decided not to be distracted. *Focus on the devil's daughter almost killing you and a helpless psycho vampire.* "He needs fresh blood—like, from a living vein—or he'll backtrack, forget how to walk, all that stuff. I've been feeding him, but guess what!"

"Oh no," she moaned.

"Can I watch?" Jon asked.

"That's right, for beating the shit out of a guest with no provocation, *and* trying to poof the vampire queen into tiny piles of ash, your grand prize is . . . letting George leech off you until all his wounds are healed! Thanks for playing."

She shuddered. "It's disgusting."

"Should have thought of that before you whaled on him." Ohhhh, Sinclair was a dark genius. This was great. She looked as appalled as I'd ever seen her.

"What if I won't do it?"

I shrugged. "Then have a nice life, and don't ever come back."

"You wouldn't! Over one of those—those things?"

"Laura."

"I'm sorry. I just don't see him the way you do. He's not a man, you know."

"Neither is the kid in the backseat—"

"Hey!"

"—but we let him hang around. Bottom line, Laura, I know I bitch about the queen gig, but the thing is, you can't just come into my house and beat the shit out of one of my vampires. You just can't. And don't pretend like you don't get it, because I know you do."

She didn't say anything. The silence got long, so Jon piped up with, "What happened after you realized you couldn't kill yourself?" and we picked up my life back in April.

CHAPTER 32

Sinclair was waiting in my room when we got back from shopping. I greeted him with a screeched, "Don't look, don't look!" as I hustled my bulging bags over to my closet, threw them in, and leaned on the door.

"Dare I guess you bought me a gift after my dreadful trespass last night?"

"If you're admitting you were an asshole, I'm not going to argue, but I felt better about you after you throttled my sister into semiconsciousness. What can I say? I'm a sucker for the old-fashioned stuff." I realized I hadn't exactly answered his question, because I added, "The thing I had on layaway was finally paid off, that's all. Don't go reading anything into it."

"You've been with Jon, then?"

I groaned miserably and sat down on the bed to pull off my shoes. "Come on, Eric! Don't start up with that tired shit again, willya? I was also with Laura, but that doesn't mean I was the *ménage* in their *trois*."

"I think you mean you were not the *trois*," he corrected. "And I was not starting up that tired shit again. My irritation with Jon now extends far beyond his romantic intentions."

"Oh yeah? God, the mind reels. What's he done now, start up with *his* tired old shit? The Bees active again?"

"No. But his current activities are almost as dangerous to you. Your life story is not appropriate for publication, in any forum."

"But it's a joke! He's passing it off as fiction, a cute idea for a classroom project. The gag is that it's supposed to be about a real person, and some of us know it is, but everybody else thinks—"

"I'm aware of the purpose of the 'gag.' Which is what he makes me want to do, by the way."

"Why, Sinclair! That was . . . dare I think the word . . . a joke? A yarn, a tale, a comical story? Are you feverish, nauseous, cramping?"

"Furthermore, I suspect he has engineered this entire thing as an excuse to stay close to you."

I sighed and stuck my shoes in my closet, fast, so Sinclair wouldn't see inside the bags.

"Elizabeth? I breathlessly await your commentary."

"What can I say? Maybe it is. Maybe it's a little weird that out of all the projects he could have thunk up, the one he picked is the one that lets him follow me around and ask questions."

"Ah." He looked at me approvingly.

"Jeez, Sinclair, I'm not a genius, but I'm not in a coma, either! I've had guys like me before; I can recognize the symptoms, poor bastards."

"Yes," he said. "We are poor bastards."

I didn't know what to say to *that,* so I just continued my train of thought. "I don't know. Maybe I feel sorry for him. Maybe I thought I owed him a break. He came all this way and basically got his heart stomped. And the whole reason he quit staking vampires was because he liked me. I felt like I had to be . . . I dunno . . ."

"Magnanimous in victory?"

I shuddered. "Of course that just came tripping off the end of your tongue, Sink Lair, what a surprise."

I noticed he was in his usual spot when we chatted: arms crossed, leaning against my door (people did have a tendency to run in after just a brief knock or worse, no knock), head tipped to one side as he listened to every word that came out of my mouth. I pulled my frog socks off and tossed them in the hamper, but at least he didn't try to move farther away when I did it. I didn't think I could take that again.

"I would almost prefer that you disliked him," he commented. "Men have been able to cajole women into bed using nothing more than their pity."

"Oh, right!" I snapped. "Like there was ever a woman in

the universe who fucked *you* because she felt sorry for you."

"I am hoping," he said, pushing away from the door and coming toward me, "there will be at least one. I behaved abominably."

"Yeah, you were a real dick." I was watching him warily. This was too good to be true! Not to mention a) nothing had changed, and b) I wasn't a faucet. "I'm glad you're sorry, but I can't just get over being upset"—I snapped my fingers—"just like that. I can't turn it on and off."

"I must beg your forgiveness," he said soberly. I realized for the first time that his hair—*his* hair—was messy, like he hadn't combed it in hours. It was as startling as if he'd gone outside without pants. "I know during lovemaking—it's the nature of vampires, I think—we have been . . . rough . . . at times, but that was no excuse for assaulting you."

"Damn right!"

"My only excuse—"

"Hey, I thought you said there *was* no excuse."

"—is that I was driven by fear, which is a new experience for me." He frowned. "An unpleasant one."

"Well." I sulked and allowed him to hug me. He did it carefully, like he was hugging a barrel of snakes. One open at both ends. "I did surprise you. And not in a good way. I really didn't mean to keep it a secret for so long, and I didn't mean to blurt it out that way."

"And you apologized, repeatedly, for that."

"Yeah, I did! What, so, you're not worried about that anymore?"

" 'That' being the frightening and unmanning way you can get into my head during our most intimate moments, while you yourself remain a locked door to me?"

"Well," I grumped, "when you have that attitude, anything's going to sound bad." Then I loosened up and kissed him on the chin. "Aw, come on. I wasn't a virgin when I met you, and I kind of liked that this was a 'first' with you. It helped me—it helped me decide a lot of things. A big thing, this October. I mean, you were aware I was going to stay with you forever, or leave forever, right?"

"Ummmm," he said, because he was nuzzling my throat. I flinched back a little, and he kissed me reassuringly in the same spot he had chomped me the night before. It had, of course, healed perfectly, but I couldn't help being twitchy.

"And part of the reason I decided to stay was because, in my head at least, you weren't sneaky and weird."

"It will take me some time," he said, working his way into my cleavage, which was as wonderful as it sounded.

"Time?" I laughed and clutched his head. "Sweetie, you're so quick to check the Book for every little thing, you forgot we're stuck with each for a thousand years."

"Anything's going to sound bad," he said, picking me up and tossing me on the bed, "when you put it like that."

CHAPTER 33

He had come up for a kiss after spending an inhuman amount of time between my legs, and I was trying to figure out if you could actually die, yes die, by orgasm. It seemed likely. It also seemed like a great way to go.

Can you hear me now?

"Sinclair, we are not doing a cell phone commercial right now," I growled. "Now take that thing and stick it in me and let's worry about something else! Anything else!"

But you can . . . pausing for the thrust. I moaned when it went home, when he buried himself in me, when I could feel him everywhere . . . *hear me.*

"Yes," I groaned. "I hear you."

And when I think about how precious you are to me and

*how I nearly broke your sister's back when I saw her sword
between your breasts, you can hear that, too?*

Thrusting back now. It was weird, having a conversation
like this. About this. But I was nothing if not adaptable.

"Yes, I hear you."

All right, then. I can live with this.

"It's nothing," I grumbled, "compared to what I have to
put up with."

"I read your columns," he said, after.

I groaned and hid myself in the blankets. After a few
seconds of digging, he found me and pulled me out. "Aha!
I've been saying that in my head for over a minute, to no
avail. So it really is only during—"

"I *told* you. Must we relive every fight, all the time?
And I don't want to hear the editorial report on my
columns."

"I liked them," he continued, ignoring my queenlike
command. And was it my imagination, or was proof that I
wasn't a constant telepath really cheering him up? "I thought
they made much sense. They will, of course, cause a bit of
a scandal among the older crowds—"

"They're not *for* the old guys. Those guys have already
figured out all the rules. I gotta admit, I kind of get a kick
out of writing them."

"Perhaps seeing the lighter side of the queen will appease
some of the more, ah, some of the vampires who are more set
in their ways. Particularly the European faction."

"I don't have any other side," I admitted. Then: "European faction?"

"Yes, that group of older vampires who was giving serious consideration to overthrowing you."

I sat up. *"What?"*

"Did you never wonder why I suddenly went to France last fall?"

"Well—yeah, but—at the time we were—I made it a point not to show too much interest in your activities because I was still mad at you for being a sneaky freak, and *this is the sort of thing I've been talking about!*"

"But I persuaded them not to revolt," he said, looking totally puzzled. "I fixed the problem for you."

"First of all, why can't they just mind their own business? They can worry about them, and I can worry about me. Jesus!"

"Because you killed two major vampires in three months, one of them the sitting power," he explained. "It was cause for concern."

"And second, *whyyyyyyyy* did you secretly go over there and then not say a word about why you were going and what happened when you got back? Instead it was all 'I miss you, Betsy, why won't you sleep with me?' "

"I did miss you," he pointed out. "And I *was* wondering why you wouldn't share my bed. Or vice versa," he added, looking down at my green flannel sheets.

"But this is the stuff I'm talking about!" I thrashed between my sheets like a landed bass. "You can't keep this shit from me!"

"But I fixed it," he said. Honest to God, he was completely bewildered. No doubt wondering why I wasn't on my knees fellating him out of pure gratitude. Men! "I fixed the problem. There was no need to bother you with any of it."

I fought not to choke the living shit out of him. "But it was *my problem*!"

"But when you didn't tell me about your sometime-telepathy—"

"That was a totally different thing! That was something I couldn't help, that I meant all along to tell you about, and eventually did, and understood why it was wrong to keep it from you, and we moved on!" I was stomping back and forth, wrapped in my comforter. "This was not sneaking off to Europe—"

"I never sneak," he said coolly.

"Oh, dude, you invented sneaking!"

"You knew where I was going. And you knew when I returned."

"Semantics! And here's a question, ladies and gentlemen—"

"Who are you talking to when you do that?"

"Why not bring me with? Huh? They were going to overthrow *me,* why not let me come over and plead my case?"

He opened his mouth. Nothing came out. I had either cornered him with my cementlike logic, or he didn't want to tell me he thought I'd fuck up the whole thing. Either way . . .

"Get out!"

"All right," he said mildly, climbing out of bed, "but you

did state in your terms that I must move all the way in, or all the way—"

"I know what I said!" I kicked the duvet in a rage. "I don't care about that now! If I look at you another second I'll— I'll kick you in the gonads! Now get lost!"

He got lost.

CHAPTER 34

"Wait a minute, wait a minute." Jessica made the time-out sign. "You made up after your other fight, but now you're fighting again?"

I nodded miserably.

"You guys. Seriously. I really think you should get married already—talk about prewedding jitters! You're tearing each other apart!"

"Perhaps my father could help," Laura suggested. "He has counseled many couples before their special day."

Oh, right. I could just see Sinclair and me sitting in the minister's office. "Thanks anyway, Laura."

"What are you doing here?" Jess demanded. She was jealous of any woman who took up my time, even relatives.

"Weren't you just here?"

"I had to let George feed again," she said glumly. She pulled back her coat sleeve to show us the neat bite marks and reddened flesh. "He's pretty much healed up now."

"Oh. Well, good work." I tried an encouraging smile, which felt like an embalmed leer. "Don't almost kill him anymore. Let that be a lesson to you. Etcetera. Time to get back to my problems: can you believe that bum?"

"Well. He *did* go to Europe to keep a bunch of scary old vampires from coming over here and killing you," Jess pointed out.

"You just like him because his rent checks have never bounced."

"No, but frankly, I figure that other hurdle—whatever it was—if you got over that, you can get over anything."

"Excuse *me*," Cathie said, right next to my ear, and I yowled and knocked over my tea. "But if we're going to get back to anyone's problems, we're getting back to mine."

"There's a ghost in the room," I told Laura and Jess.

"Oh, honey. Not this again." Jess didn't believe in ghosts (funny 'tude for someone who lived with vampires). No matter what I did, I couldn't get her to see them. So she just . . .

"I'm out of here." She got up, ready to put her cup and saucer in the sink, when Laura opened her mouth. I shook my head, and we sat in silence until Jessica left.

"What does it want?" Laura practically whispered.

"I can hear *her* fine," Cathie snapped.

"She can hear you fine," I translated. "She's the latest victim of the Driveway Killer."

"The one who's missing? Mrs. Scoman?"

"There's another one?" Cathie cried. "Dammit, dammit! This is why I'm floating around this dump, trying you to get your head out of your ass! This is exactly what I was trying to prevent! Son of a fucking bitch!"

"All *right,* don't *yell.*" I put my hands over my face and shivered for a minute. "She's mad because there's another victim."

"Well . . . another lady who's missing. She got pulled out of her driveway tonight; they've already put an alert out on her." Laura was obviously trying to sound encouraging to the dead woman she couldn't see or hear. "She hasn't actually shown up, um, dead."

"Then let's go get him! Right now!"

"She wants to go after the bad guy," I told Laura.

"Of course she does! It's Mrs. Robinson, right?"

"Yeah, yeah, let's go!"

"Wait wait *wait.*" Cathie, halfway through the wall, backed up and looked at me. Laura, halfway to the door, also stopped. "Where are you guys going? Do you know where he lives? All Cathie knows is that she got conked in her driveway— that's not exactly news. And she has a vague idea of being in 'some old house' and then she woke up dead. We have to tell Nick all this stuff—"

"How?" Laura asked. "Of course, you're right, we must tell the law, but how will we explain our knowledge?"

"We could say we got an anonymous letter or something."

"Which he will then wish to see." Laura sounded apologetic to be thinking up problems. "At least, I know I would."

"A phone call?"

"Why would they call you? Or me, for that matter?"

"Because Jessica's going out with him?"

"You could pretend to be a victim who got away," Laura suggested, "and then tell them everything the ghost tells you."

"That's not bad," Cathie said, "but there's no damn *time*. Don't you get it? He doesn't keep us very long; he's scared."

"Scared of getting caught?" I asked, *so* far over my head.

"No, scared of us. The victims. He'll kill her tonight and dump her in some awful public parking lot where everyone will see her naked and laugh and point."

"Nobody—" I began, shocked.

"No, that's what *he* thinks. It's what he wants. Now can we come up with how to explain it *later*? At least let's go drive to where I remember the house!"

"An address, anything?"

"No, but at least we can get in the area. Maybe I'll remember more. It's worth doing, goddammit!"

"You're right," I said, after I'd told Laura everything that had been said. "It's worth doing."

"Now, now, *right now*!"

"She's right," Laura said, and I assumed it was in response to what I had said, not because she could hear Cathie. "It's worth doing. Let's go at once."

CHAPTER 35

"Bad bad bad bad bad bad bad bad *bad BAD* idea," I said again.

"Take a left," Cathie commanded from the back. "And enough complaining. I'm sick to death of the complaining."

"We're not cops! Okay? In this car is a secretary, a college student, and a part-time horse trainer."

"It would have been full-time," Laura said, "but now that I'm dead, that bum Gerry's gonna snake the slot right out from under me."

"We should have told Nick the whole thing and let him come into the neighborhood with about nine SWAT teams."

"Never mind how difficult that would be to explain," Laura began.

"Right, and scare the killer off with a bunch of uniforms running around!" Cathie snapped. "No, we have to catch that jerk. Driveway Killer . . . Driveway Asshole is more like it. Left!"

"Does anything look familiar to her?" Laura asked.

"No," Cathie said. "But I won't forget the smell in a hurry. It stank like nothing else has."

"He stank?"

"No, the neighborhood. Something chemical, something like—"

"The Glazier Refinery?" I read off the sign as we passed it. There were about two hundred smokestacks in the air, and they were all pouring out smoke that smelled like fake pizza.

Cathie retched in my backseat. Could ghosts puke? I tried to stay focused. "I guess this is the area."

"God, that smell! How could the cops not smell it on my— goddammit, because he strips them and then dumps them."

"Still, you'd think there'd be some clues," I said doubtfully.

"This isn't *CSI*," Laura said, watching out the window. "Not that I watch the show—an hour of people finding new and interesting ways to kill each other? No thank you. But this is real life, not television. And it's a big metro area. Millions of people, doing millions of things, over a large square area. I've lived out here all my life, and I've never even heard of this place. I think when we catch him, it will be obvious what he was doing and where he was taking them, but we have to get him first."

"Whoa, whoa! You guys, I think we agreed—"

"I didn't agree to anything," Cathie said.

"—that this is a fact-finding mission. We're not here to bust the guy. We need something concrete to take back to Nick and then *they* can come get him. We're just nosing around for clues."

"And if we find him standing over a woman with a big butcher knife?" Laura asked.

"Actually," Cathie piped up helpfully, "he strangles us. With his belt."

I shuddered. "If worse comes to worst, we'll catch him. Don't sweat it, Cathie, Laura and I are totally capable of knocking a guy out and calling the cops. I'll distract him by letting him stab me multiple times and then Laura will kick the shit out of him. We'll just use a nearby phone and do the anonymous tip thing. If Mrs.—uh—"

"Scoman. You really are terrible with names," Laura chided me gently.

"I know. Anyway, if she needs to go to the hospital, we'll take her. We'll—look, we're putting the cart ahead of the horse, here. Let's see if we can find the damn house first."

"He took off his belt, and he strangled me until I shit myself." I was shocked to see Cathie had scooted way over and was whispering in Laura's ear. "He did it because he's weak and because he's afraid of women. And after I was dead, he took off all my clothes and made fun of my boobs."

"Cathie! I mean, jeez, I'm not saying you don't have a right, but cripes!"

"What?" Cathie was smack in my rearview mirror again. "I didn't say anything. I'm looking at houses."

"I heard her that time!" Laura said, excited. "Talking about her boobs and such. I think I'm getting a new power!"

"No," I said, kicking myself for ever thinking things were as bad as they could get. "I think your mother's here."

"What?"

"Surprise," Cathie said, and smiled.

"Mother!" Laura had twisted around in her seat and was glaring at the devil. "I can do this without your help!"

"I'm sure you can," the devil went on in Cathie's voice, smirking with Cathie's face. "But it seemed for a moment like you were going to take the coward's way out. Knocking him out and waiting for the police . . ." The devil rolled her eyes. "That's just sad."

"Go to Hell," Laura said through gritted teeth, and—I'm not how she did this from the passenger seat of a Dodge Stratus—pulled out her sword and stabbed Cathie with it.

Who promptly cried, "What the hell do you think you're doing, you morbid bitch?"

Laura looked at me. "Is she talking again?"

"Oh, yeah."

"Good." The sword disappeared. Laura turned back around. Nobody said a word for five miles.

CHAPTER 36

"Your sword disrupts magic," I began, because somebody had to say something.

"Yes."

"So why didn't it 'kill' Cathie?"

"I don't know. I've only ever killed vampires with it. I tried to kill a werewolf once, but it just made her change back into a woman. She was so startled she ran away from me, and I never saw her again."

"There are werewolves?" Cathie asked. "For real?"

"You gotta be kidding me, werewolves. Like I don't have enough to deal with?" I bitched.

"It was only the one time," Laura said defensively. "I'm

sure you'll never have to meet one. They're rarer than vampires, I bet."

"Let's for cripe's sake hope so. Cathie, is any of this looking familiar?"

"I only saw the house from the inside," she said apologetically. "I remember what the inside looked like . . . and the smell of the place. I remember that."

"Oh, it's that one." Laura pointed to a nondescript split-level on the end of the block. It was tan with dark-brown trim. The driveway and sidewalks had been neatly shoveled.

"It is?" Cathie whispered, leaning forward so that her head popped through the seat between us.

"How do you know? Cathie, does anything ring a bell?"

"Just the smell. How does she know?"

Laura sighed, a dreadful sound, and looked at the nice little split-level the way I would look at a child abuser. "Is it a black house? All black, even the sidewalks? Even the snow around it?"

"No," Cathie and I said in unison.

"It looks black to me," Laura said simply.

CHAPTER 37

"Hi, Eric? It's Betsy. Listen, don't freak out, but Laura and Cathie—never mind, long story—anyway, we think we've found where the Driveway Killer lives, so we're going to check it out. It's 4241 Treadwell Lane in Minneapolis. Anyway, when you get this, call me. Except I'm going to have my ringer turned off so we can sneak up on this guy if we have to, so don't flip out if I don't answer. Okay, love you, bye!"

"Are you happy now?" Cathie bitched. "Can you please get off your ass and help me, or do you have more calls to make?"

"Hey, you've seen the horror movies. The heroine never tells anyone where she's going—it's maddening. Or if she does remember she has a cell phone, it's always dead. Or she can't get a signal."

"Or her fiancé is on the other line and doesn't answer the call," Laura prompted helpfully.

"You shut up. And keep that thing put away unless we need it."

"We'd better not need it," she said as we parked a few blocks away and got out of the car. "It only disrupts magic; it doesn't do squat on regular people. Well, humans, I mean."

"Oh."

"I've been meaning to ask," she whispered as we snuck up on the split-level and Cathie ran through (literally through) snowbanks ahead imploring us to hurry, hurry, hurry! "I thank God every night that I didn't hurt you, but, uh, *why* didn't my sword hurt you? It should have killed you."

I shrugged. "Got no idea, doll. But one thing at a time."

"Oh. All right."

"Now remember," I whispered as we peeked into the front window. "Fact-finding. And if the woman's here, we'll save her."

"What if there's no woman here, just the bad guy?" Laura asked.

"You'll recognize him, right?" I asked Cathie.

"Too damned right I will."

"Okay, well, then we'll pull back and call the good guys and wait for them to come."

"What if he leaves before—"

"One thing at a time, okay? We don't even know if anybody's home."

"Nobody's in the living room," Laura observed.

"Just a minute," Cathie said, and flitted through the window. We hid (in plain sight, in the front yard), feeling like idiots (at least I did) while she phased through the house. She popped out through the garage and said, "He's not here. But there's a woman in the basement!"

"Pull up the garage door," Laura suggested.

"Everything's locked," Cathie fretted.

"I'm sure I can pull it up—" I began.

"But you guys," Laura protested, "he'll *see* it!"

"Who cares? Do him good to get a really big scare. Maybe he'll do something stupid."

"And maybe he'll run away and we won't catch him."

"Well, we can't just leave that poor woman down in the dark by herself, thinking she's going to die."

"Goddamned right!" Cathie said. "One of you break something and get in here! All I can do is float around going *boooooooooo*. Cross of Christ!"

I picked up one of the bricks lining the sidewalk and tossed it through the front window. The noise was tremendous. Not to mention the mess. Cathie and Laura stared at me, shocked.

"Maybe this way, he'll think it's just kids." It was lame, but it was all I had. "Maybe he won't think the cops are here if he just sees a broken window."

"Oh. Good one." Cathie floated approvingly away, and Laura carefully hoisted herself up and into the living room.

"Watch the glass," I warned her and then cut myself a good one and cursed. Luckily, I bled as well as I read: sluggishly.

"Down here!" Cathie called, and darted into a closed wooden door.

What's funny was, I was starting to get used to the smell of the refinery—we'd been driving around the neighborhood a good twenty minutes, after all. But Cathie was right, it blotted out everything else. If he was killing women in the basement, I couldn't smell it from the kitchen. I couldn't even smell the kitchen from the kitchen.

Laura and I hurried down the stairs, which were predictably dark and spooky until Laura found the light switch. Banks of fluorescents winked on, and in the far corner, we could see a woman with messy, short blond hair, tied up and gagged with electrician's tape. Her outfit was, needless to say, a mess.

"Ha!" Cathie screeched, phasing though the wood-burning furnace and zooming around in a tight circle. "Told you, told you!"

"It's all right," Laura said, going to her. "You're safe now. Er, this might sting a bit." And she ripped the tape off the woman's mouth. "It's like a Band-Aid," she told her. "You can't do it little by little."

"He's coming back—to kill me—" Mrs. Scoman (I assume it was Mrs. Scoman) gasped. "He said he—was going to use his special friend—and kill me—" Then she leaned over and barfed all over Laura's shoes.

"That's all right," Laura said, rubbing the terrified woman's back. "You've had a hard night."

"If those were my shoes," I muttered to Cathie, "I wouldn't be able to be so nice about it."

"Oh, your sister's a freak," Cathie said, dismissing ShoeGate with a wave of her hand. "I've only known her a couple of days, and I figured that one out."

"She's different and nice," I said defensively, "but that doesn't make her a freak."

"Trust me. Having been killed by one, I recognize the breed."

"You take that back! You can't put someone like Laura in the same league as the Driveway Asshole."

"Will you two stop it?" Laura hissed, struggling with the tape. "You're scaring poor Mrs. Scoman! And I am not in the same league as the Driveway Asshole."

"I just want to get out of here," she groaned. "I want to get out of here so bad. Just my feet. I don't care about my hands. I can run with my hands tied."

Then I heard it. "Move," I told Laura. "The—we have to go now."

Cathie darted up through the ceiling.

"What?" Laura asked.

I started to rip through the tape with a couple tugs, tricky because I didn't want to hurt Mrs. Scoman. "The garage door just went up," I said shortly.

Cathie swooped back into the basement. "He's back! And boy, he is freaked out. Keeps muttering about the damn foster kids, whatever that's supposed to mean."

"Hurry," Mrs. Scoman whispered.

"Please don't throw up on me. If I do it any faster or harder, I could break all the bones in your hands."

"I don't care! Do my feet! *Break* my feet! Cut them off if you have to, just *get me out of here*!"

"Carrie? Do you have friends downstairs, Carrie?"

"Oh, great," I mumbled. "The predictably creepy killer has arrived."

Cathie pointed at the man—I couldn't see him because we were as much under the stairs as beside them—walking down the stairs. "Time's up, motherfucker," was how she greeted him, and damn, I liked the woman's style.

"Why did no one think to bring a knife?" Laura asked the air.

"Because we're the hotshit vampire queen and devil's daughter, and we don't need knives. Unless, of course, the bad guy ties up his victims with *tape*. Then we're screwed." Ah! I finally got her feet free and went to work on her hands. Because she would have had to run past the killer to escape, I shoved her back down when she tried to scramble to her feet. "It's okay," I told her. "We've got it covered. We really are the hotshit—never mind. I'll have this off in another minute."

The killer turned and came into the basement. Saw us. (Well, most of us . . . not Cathie.) Looked startled, then quickly recovered. "Carrie, I told you, no friends over on a school night."

"My name isn't Carrie," Mrs. Scoman whispered. She wouldn't look at the killer.

Cathie stepped into his chest and stood inside him. "Asshole. Jerkoff. Tyrant. Fuckwad," she informed him from inside his own head. "Loser. Virgin. Dimwit. Asshat. God, what I wouldn't give to be corporeal right now!"

"It's overrated," I mumbled.

"I can't believe this loser's *face* was the last thing I saw."

"You aren't the foster kids," the psycho nutjob killer said, looking puzzled. "I thought the kids at the end of the block broke my window again."

"Score," I said under my breath, tugging away. "What did I say? Huh?"

"Yeah, you actually had a good idea," Cathie snarked. "And we're not calling the police right this second why again?"

"Why did you kill those women?" Laura asked, the way you'd ask someone why they picked a red car over a blue one. "Why did you steal Mrs. Scoman?"

"Because they're mine," he explained, the way you'd explain about owning a shirt. Everyone was being all calm and civilized, and it was freaking me the hell out. I could smell trouble. Not a huge talent, given the circumstances, but it was still making me twitchy as a cat in heat. "They're all mine. Carrie forgot, so I have to keep reminding her."

"Psycho!" I coughed into my fist.

"Did you really," Laura began, and then had to try again, "did you really strangle them until they pooped, and then make fun of them after you stole their clothes?"

"Laura, he's crazy. You're not going to get a straight answer. Look at him!"

Unfortunately, looking at him didn't help: he looked like a lawyer on casual Fridays. Nice, clean blue work shirt.

Khakis. Penny loafers. Not at all like the slobbering nutjob he obviously was.

Then he fucked himself forever by saying, "It sucks when you get the bra off and find out they don't have a decent rack. I don't mind them lying about that other stuff, but tell the truth about your tits, that's what my dad used to say. Otherwise, it's like lying."

Then, of course, he was dead, because Laura leaned down, picked up a chunk of wood off the pile, and broke his head in half. I screamed. Mrs. Scoman screamed. Even Cathie screamed, but I think she was happy. I wasn't. I was in Hell. I think Mrs. Scoman thought so, too.

CHAPTER 38

I used my vampire mojo to convince Mrs. Scoman she had escaped and had no idea why the killer was dead, or who had killed him. I reminded her to tell Nick and the task force the killer's address. We thought she'd make out okay . . . none of the killer's blood was on her. It was all over Laura.

"Okay," I said on the way home. "I'm a little concerned."

"I lost my temper," Laura said, looking out the window. "I'll be the first to admit it."

"Freak!" Cathie sang from the backseat.

"That's another thing," I snapped, glaring into the rearview mirror. "You're supposed to disappear and be in heaven or wherever you people go after I've fixed your problem."

"Yeah, I know, but I kind of like this."

"What?"

"This." She waved her ghostly hands through my head. I shuddered, and the car swerved. "How cheated was I? Repeat after me: promising life cut short."

"Yeah, but . . ." I paused delicately. "You're dead. It's time to move on."

"Look who's talking. Besides, I helped you, right? I could get into the house when you guys were standing out on the lawn like jerks. I think I could be pretty good at this. Anyway, I think I'll hang around."

"Oh, Christ on crackers."

"What?"

"Good to have you aboard!" I said with fake heartiness.

"She's still here?" Laura asked. "That's odd."

"Don't try to change the subject! You murdered that guy. He was just standing there, and you killed him!"

"Killed him dead," Cathie agreed. "Like a big blond roach motel. She's a freak, but I'm totally in love with your sister right now."

"You stay out of this."

"If you think about it, the whole thing is kind of my fault," Cathie confessed.

"Never mind! Laura, what were you thinking?"

"That I was very very very very angry? And it upset me to know he would be walking around breathing the same air as my folks?"

Points for honesty, at least. "Laura, it's like this. I don't know if you're having a bad month, or if certain prophecies are coming to light, or what, but I gotta admit, I'm concerned. Okay? I mean, I'm a vampire and I'm not going around— okay, I am, but that's a totally different thing."

"I know it was wrong," Laura said, looking at me with guileless blue eyes, "but you have to admit, it will be difficult for him to take off his belt and strangle any more women after today. Won't it?" She almost smiled, and was that a flash of green I saw in her eyes?

I decided it was my imagination.

Before I could take the issue further—not that I had the slightest idea what to say, not exactly having the moral high ground—the blue Mustang behind me flashed its high beams twice. Then it snuggled right up on my bumper, and my cell phone vibrated.

"Do they give dead people speeding tickets?" Cathie asked.

"That's no cop, that's my fiancé." I hummed the first few lines of "My Boyfriend's Back" and then answered the phone.

CHAPTER 39

"Eric, it was just an ordinary guy this time! It's not like I got tricked by vampires or got stuck in the middle of another coup."

He put his hands behind his back. I knew why; it was so he wouldn't choke me. "What is this aversion you have to waiting for my assistance?"

"It's not aversion. You're just never around when I need you. Hum. Okay, that sounded nicer in my head. Hey, I did call you. It's not my fault you didn't answer your cell."

"I was available twenty seconds later! You were physically unable to wait less than half a minute?"

"Well, I kind of wish we had, because the thing is . . ." I burst into tears.

"Oh, Elizabeth, don't do that." He snuggled me into his arms. "Was I shouting? I won't apologize for worrying, but I will clarify: I was concerned, not angry."

"It's not that. Laura—she killed the bad guy."

"And that's . . . er, bad?"

"It's how she did it. He didn't even attack us or anything. He was just standing there. And there were all these piles of wood in the basement, because he has—had—a wood-burning stove, and she leaned over and picked up a big old chunk of wood, and just *beaned* him with it! And I heard the crack— I heard his head break!" I shuddered. "And brains—did you know brains are pink and red? Don't answer that," I ordered tearfully. "And all this *stuff* came out. And he was just . . . dead. And she didn't even care! Just said later that she lost her temper."

"That . . . is cause for concern," he said after a moment's thought. "I must admit, I have . . . dispatched . . . my share of societal burdens in my day. But Laura seems to be—"

"Going over to the dark side."

"Or something," he agreed. "But it could be argued that she saved lives."

"Definitely it could be argued. I guess Driveway Jerk had this thing for short-haired blondes because when he was a teen, this girl named—never mind, it's creepy and stupid at the same time. And he was just driving around, looking for the right type to be in the right spot at the right time! Tell me how *that* can be allowed to happen in a sane world. You could be putting your groceries away ten minutes later and not be killed."

"But you and Laura are in a sane world," he suggested. "Righting wrongs."

"I really don't think this is the tactic we should use when talking to her about this, okay?" I pulled away so I could look into his eyes. "And see this? How I came right home and told you everything and we're discussing it like sane people who talk to each other?"

"Well, I did follow you to be sure you were going to do that," he admitted.

"This, *this* is what couples do! *Kuh-MYUN-ih-kate*. Memorize the word, Sinclair. Practice it."

"Consider me chastened." He didn't look terribly repentant, though. "Getting back to the matter of your sister . . ."

"I don't know what to do. What can I tell her, killing is wrong? Of course it's wrong, everybody knows that. She knows it, too. The problem is, that only makes us the biggest hypocrites in the world. Not to mention, it's not like she killed a Girl Scout. She did the world a favor. So what do I say to her?"

"That you're watching," he said quietly. "We're all watching."

"I think I'll take the 'we'll be there for you' tactic on that one."

"Either way. Come here, now, darling, sit down." He rubbed my shoulders, and I sat on the bed. "You've had a tough week, haven't you?"

"It's my new worst week ever," I sniveled.

"Well, in light of our new 'tell all' policy, I have some news for you."

I sighed and rested my forehead on his shoulder. "Who's dead now?"

"The *Star Tribune* has picked up your 'Dear Betsy' column."

"What?" I jerked my head up. "There've only been, what? Two newsletters? And I thought that was impossible! Anybody seeing the newsletter!"

"Supposedly it was. Marjorie is beside herself. Heads will roll, I can assure you. Possibly literally. We suspect either a member of the *Tribune* payroll is a vampire, or an enterprising human hacked into her system and gave it to a reporter."

"So what's—what's going to happen?"

"Fortunately, feedback seems to be that it's not to be taken seriously. The editor thinks it is a joke, the readers seem to like it, and the readers who are vampires are keeping their mouths shut."

"So only a few people in the city know it's a real letter to real vampires?"

"Yes. And because Marjorie's discretion is on the line, she is moving heaven and earth to find out who is responsible. I imagine we'll have some answers on that in a short time."

"Well . . . I guess things could be worse."

"They are about to get that way, I assure you."

I groaned and flopped down on the bed. "This whole tell-each-other-everything debacle, you're punishing me for it now, aren't you?"

"Darling, you know I live to obey your slightest whim. When before, I sought to protect you from the problems of governing a nation, now I see it was merely my ham-handed way of repressing you. Well, those days are over!" he declared, over my moans of horror. "Whereas in the past I felt discretion was the better part of valor—"

"Oh, now you're just making shit up to fuck with me."

"—now all must be revealed, constantly."

"Look, I figured out that you don't keep things from me to be mean. You just can't help it."

"Ah, but starting now, I shall help it."

"I get that you think solving problems for me proves your worth."

He sniffed. "I wouldn't go *that* far."

"You can't help it, you're in *lurrrrrvvv*."

"Stop that. I was going to tell you, Jon has transcribed nearly the entire first draft of your little tell-all."

"I thought it was going to be, like, a paper."

"It's turning into a book, dear. Three hundred pages at last count."

"Oh, he told you this?"

"It's possible I had Tina hack into his Sidekick," he admitted.

"Nice! Well, this is nothing new, right?"

"Given the fallout from the *Tribune* picking up your column—"

"What fallout? I thought everybody agreed it was a joke."

"—I got Jon alone and convinced him he had never written

the book, never had the idea, never had any interest in your life story."

"Oh, Christ."

"Then I erased it."

"Oh, Sinclair. Oh, boy." I put my hands over my eyes. "This is going to be a bad one."

"You may proceed," he said, "with the yelling."

I tried to get myself under control. *He did it out of love. Misguided, weird love, but love. He's trying to protect you. In a misguided, weird way.*

"Okay, Eric, that was bad. Pretty bad. And I think, after what Jon has done for us, I think you should undo your mojo."

"But I went to all that trouble," he explained patiently, like I didn't get what he had done, "to be sure he forgot everything."

"And now I want you to make him remember! Look, he'll flunk his class, among other things. You really want him moping around here because he got an F in bio or whatever the hell it's called? And second, I agreed to let him do this. So by you sneaking in and undoing it, I look bad. Really, really bad."

He looked at me for a long minute. "I admit," he said at last, "I had not considered it in those terms. Your authority should not be undermined. Even by me."

Especially by you, but that was a topic for another time.

"So you'll undo it?"

"I will try," he said. "And in the spirit of full revelation,

I must tell you I'm not sure it will work. I've never tried to undo a mojo, as you call it."

"What, in your whole life you've never made a mistake?"

He smiled. "No, but no one ever asked me to go back and try to rectify my errors. No one ever dared."

"Probably why you've got such an attitude problem."

"Probably," he agreed, and pulled me into his arms.

I wriggled around until I was straddling him. "I don't know about you, but I haven't eaten in days."

"You've been busy," he said, and then he groaned as I found his zipper and pulled. "I must say, I didn't think I would enjoy this full disclosure rule you've implemented . . . ah . . . don't stop doing that . . ."

"Aren't you funny," I said.

"Consider it an order from your king."

"I'm hysterical with laughter here." I wiggled down, pulled down his pants as I went, and divested him of his socks. Frantic, I yanked at his black boxer shorts until they were little cotton shreds, took his dick in my hand, moved it out of my way, and bit him right on his femoral artery.

His hands plunged into my hair and he made fists, almost hard enough to hurt, but not quite. He was so good at that. At coming up to the line but not crossing it. I tried not to think of all the practice he must have had to get so good.

His cool, salty blood nearly overflowed my mouth, and for the first time in days, I wasn't morbidly thirsty. Instead I drank from him and felt his cock pulse in my hand, felt him give way, felt him helpless, literally helpless in my hand as he spurted all over the sheets, as he gave control to me.

I love you. Love you. Love you.

And the worst week ever was redeemed.

CHAPTER 40

"Look, you don't even have to *go* to the florist, okay? I've got a book full of pictures for you to look at."

"Darling, I trust your taste impeccably. I'm sure whatever you choose will be appropriate to the . . . lovely occasion."

"You're lying! You think I keep my taste in my butt!"

"I am certain," Sinclair said, totally straight-faced, "that I never used that phrase."

Tina, who had been coming into the kitchen to get God-knows-what, abruptly turned around.

"Freeze!" I shouted. "I've got a bone to pick with you, too."

"How can I serve you, my queen?" she asked, all innocent. When she wanted, she could look like a sixteen-year-old kid.

"How about not hacking into my friend's computers and helping Sinclair *eat* three hundred pages? How about that?"

Tina looked over at Sinclair, who had suddenly rediscovered that the *Wall Street Journal* printed stock prices. No help there.

"Look, I know you're the king's man—er, so to speak— and you feel like you can't say no to him, but—"

"It's not that."

"What?"

"Not entirely that," she amended. "If I may be frank, Majesty, I don't think his little school project was at all appropriate. You do have enemies, you know."

"Tell me about it." I glared at the two of them, the undead Frick and Frack.

"I mean human enemies. Why make things easier for them? There is a difference between dishonesty and discretion."

Oh, like either of those two would know. "Look, just leave my friend's stuff alone, okay? I've already talked to Sinclair about this, and he's going to undo the 'you are getting verrrrrrry sleeeeeepy' thing."

"He is?"

"I am," Sinclair said to the paper.

"Love," Tina said, gaping. "It's truly an amazing thing to behold."

"Shush, Tina."

"My king." Fighting a smile, she grabbed the mail and walked out.

"As for you. You don't even have to pick the flowers you like, okay? Just pick the ones you absolutely loathe, can't stand the sight of, and I'll be sure those aren't anywhere near you on the big day."

"Darling," he said, turning the page, "I just don't have intensely strong feelings for flowers."

"But you were raised on a farm! You must have *some* preferences."

"Darling, I have a penis. Ergo I have no preferences."

"When are you and your penis going to get with the program?" Jessica asked, coming in the door Tina had just left by. "Just do what she asks, and it'll all be over that much sooner. For everybody."

"Way to make it sound fun, Jess."

"It's *not* fun, Bets. Not for anyone but you." She pulled up a chair and sat down. Eric was looking at her with some interest.

"At last," he said. "Someone says it out loud."

"Eric, she's been planning this wedding since she was in the seventh grade. Honest to God. She used to bring *Brides* magazine to study hall, and she'd show me the dress, the tux, the cake, the flowers. She even had the name of your kids picked out. She *still* does that."

"Hey, hey," I protested. "I haven't looked at an issue of *Brides* in years. A year. Six months. Look, let's get back on track, all right? Sinclair? You look okay? You're kind of pale, even for you."

"No, no, I'm fine." He managed a smile. He *had* looked

sort of ghastly while Jessica was laying it out. "You realize, after this . . . wedding . . . you'll also be 'Sinclair.'"

Oh. My. God. I actually had managed to put that *huge* problem out of my mind. It was easy, what with the ghosts and cops and serial killers on my radar. But now, it was *baaaaaack,* looming in my head like a big dead flower. For a second I was totally horrified. Then I recovered. "No, I won't. I'm keeping my name."

"No, you are *not.*"

"Like hell!"

"Uh-oh," Jessica muttered.

"If I have to go through this farcical event, the very damned least you can do is be Mrs. Elizabeth Sinclair."

"What does *farcical* mean?" I asked suspiciously.

"Happy," Jessica said.

"Oh. Okay. Look, Sinclair, I realize, being a million years old, that you can't help being an ancient disgusting chauvinist pig. But you're just gonna have to get over it in this case, because this is the twenty-first century, in case you haven't noticed, and women don't have to submerge their identities with their husband's."

"The entire point of getting married," Sinclair began, "is to—" He cut himself off and tilted his head to the left. Jessica turned and looked, too. I couldn't understand what the fuss was about; it was Laura. She was, despite recent events, welcome in our home anytime.

She eased the kitchen doors open and stepped in. "*Helloooo?* May I come in?"

Jessica was staring. "What are *you* doing here?"

Then I realized. It was Saturday night. Laura always went to Mass on Saturday nights. Said it kept her out of trouble, plus she could sleep late the next day.

She shrugged and pulled up a chair. "Oh, you know. I just—didn't feel like going tonight."

I was trying not to stare, and failing. "For the first time *ever*. Your folks are gonna kill me! They're gonna think I'm a bad influence."

"You are," Jessica said.

"It's no big deal, everyone. Maybe I'll go tomorrow."

"Forgive us for staring," Sinclair said. "It's just that you are so . . . devout. It was a surprise, seeing you here when you are usually . . . elsewhere."

"It's no big deal," she said again, and everyone heard the warning that time.

Luckily (?), George the Fiend chose that moment to also walk into the kitchen. I guess we were having a party and nobody told me.

"Now what's *he* doing up here?" Jessica asked. "To think, I almost didn't come in here for a glass of milk. Look at all the stuff I would have missed."

"I dunno," I said, staring. George was dragging half the blanket he'd crocheted, hopped up on a kitchen stool, drank all my tea—the first time he'd evinced evidence in anything but blood—spat it out on the floor in disgust, and started crocheting again.

Laura cleared her throat. "I, ah, want to take this chance,

Mr. George, to apologize for—for what I did the other night. I was picking a fight because I was angry at someone else, and that's a poor excuse. In fact, it's no excuse. So again, I apologize. I'm very, very sorry. And I'm sorry to you, too, Betsy, and you, Eric, for laying hands on one of your subjects."

I shrugged it off with a mumbled "Well, what are ya gonna do?" but Sinclair, doubtless used to this sort of thing, waved it off with a kingly, "Think no more of it, Laura, dear. We know your actions are normally above reproach."

Yeah. Normally.

"He seemed better after I fed him," Laura suggested.

I restrained the impulse to slap my forehead. Of course he was better, duh! He got better after drinking my blood—queen's blood. How much good would the devil's bloodline do him? He could probably do my taxes by now.

"That's the stuff I got him last week," Jessica said, staring at the lavender blanket, which was almost as big as my bed. "He must be just about out. I'll run over to the fabric store and get him some more."

"Red, please," George the Fiend said.

Pandemonium. Chaos. And no matter what we tempted him with, how much we cajoled, how often Sinclair ordered, or how often I begged, he didn't say another word.

CHAPTER 41

"Is this the third date? Or the fourth?"

"Nosy bitch," Jessica laughed. She checked her diamond earrings for the twentieth time.

"Yes," I assured her. "They're still there." I'd been saving to get her the matching pendant at Tiffany's; the classic blue box was on the swag-draped parlor mantel right this minute.

Okay, Sinclair was helping me. Not that he was big into Christmas. But he liked the idea of giving Jessica an extravagant gift. It would be the first time we gave anybody a present together. "You look like a tasteful Christmas tree."

"Meaning my ass looks fat in this green dress."

"No, no. You just look very spirit-of-the-seasony."

"Did you ever figure out what to give Sinclair?"

"Yeah. I took back asking him to un-mojo Jon."

"So now Jon will"—Jessica thought this out—"not remember he wrote the book about you."

"Right. I mean, it's a rotten thing to do, but I can't just think of myself on this one. There's a bunch of vampires counting on me to look out for them—I finally figured that out when I saved George from Laura. Well, a few days after I saved George from Laura. Even if they don't know I'm looking out for them, I'm supposed to be. So . . . no book of my life."

"Well, if that's what being the queen means to you, then, because you're the queen, I guess that's it."

"Yeah, that's it. I mean, I can hardly marry Sinclair and protect vampires *and* not be the queen. Even for me, that's pretty stupid."

"*Stupid*'s a harsh word," she said absently, fluffing her lashes with mascara.

"Isn't Jon supposed to turn in his bio after Christmas break?"

"Yeah." I laughed evilly. "Sinclair's doing it for him. He'd better not fob it off on Tina, either. A history of the life and times of Grover Cleveland. Apparently Sinclair knew him." I laughed harder. The perfect punishment!

"You talk it out with Laura yet?"

"No." I quit laughing. "I don't know what to say without sounding like a jerk. I guess—I guess we're just hoping it was a slip. I mean, look who her mom is. She's bound to have a short temper. And it's not like the guy didn't have it coming."

"Is that what the party line is? He had it coming?"

"No," I almost snapped, "but it's the best I can do. I don't see Nick crying about it."

"Big-time promotion, probably," she admitted. "And that's what we're celebrating. The Task Force is just about done. Nick's going back to his everyday stuff. And the Driveway Killer's done. And the Scomans are going to have a great Christmas."

"Assuming she ever stops having nightmares."

"Your little ghost told you that? What a voyeur."

"I heard that!" Cathie said, and then popped back out, probably to nag (not that they could hear her) the guys putting up the tree. We were late with it this year, and out of deference to Sinclair and Tina, Jess, Marc, and I didn't join in the trimming festivities. It had been a big enough fight just letting Jessica order one and have it sent to the house.

Needless to say, those two would be avoiding the entire east wing of the house until after New Year's.

"Obviously, if she'd had to pick between her life and nightmares, it's an easy choice. Still, I wish we could have spared her the entire experience."

"Come on. You saved her. And the bad guy got his. And you're getting married! Probably."

"What?"

"Well, I'm pretty sure. And I'm finally getting laid."

"It's a Christmas miracle," I said with mock joy. "With devils and vampires and dead serial killers."

"It's just gotten so commercial," she agreed, touching up

her lipstick. "Want to sneak down and put a cross on the tree later?"

"No, I'd better not. Poor things, they've already got the heebie-jeebies."

"Boy, there's a phrase I never thought would be associated with bad-ass vampires."

"Any kind of vampires. Anyway. We'll work on that for next year. If they're going to stay out of the room altogether, why *not* put a cross on the tree?"

She laughed and slung a black cashmere wrap over her bony shoulders. "Good point. Now, on a scale of one to ten, with one being ratty-ass you, and ten being Halle Berry—"

"Nine point six. Definitely."

"What a liar you are, my girl." She kissed me, leaving an orange smear on my cheek, and floated out on a cloud of Chanel.

CHAPTER 42

And I in my kerchief, and Ma in her cap . . . that was all of it I knew, unfortunately. My mom could recite the whole thing by heart, all twenty verses or however many there were. Jess, Marc, Jon, and I were heading over there tomorrow night for Christmas Eve dinner. She'd tell it to me then.

I shut my—our—bedroom door behind me and saw Sinclair in a miserable huddle in the middle of the bed. "It's here now, isn't it?" he asked. "I can feel it. Draining the strength from me."

"Oh, jeez, you're such a baby! It's just a Christmas tree. It's not a nuclear device."

He shuddered. "You say tomato, I say *toe-mah-toe.*"

"It's not even that big!" I held my hand up to my waist.

"It's only like this big. We had to put most of the decorations back in the attic."

"It's going down the day after tomorrow, right?"

"It just went up! Oh, while I'm thinking of it, I don't suppose you want to go to you-know-what Eve dinner tomorrow with my mom."

He grimaced, like he smelled something bad. "Your mother is a charming woman in all ways, and normally I would be delighted."

"Thanks but no thanks, huh?"

"I am not leaving this house until the twenty-sixth."

"You guys. I swear."

"You will never understand, which is both boggling and frightening."

"Uh-huh. You're probably too freaked to get it up, am I right?"

He cocked an eyebrow at me. "Not quite that freaked out."

EPILOGUE

"Thanks for not un-hypnotizing Jon," I said drowsily, much later.

His chest rumbled beneath my cheek as he laughed. "Which reminds me, my report on President Cleveland is nearly finished."

"Ha! Serves you right. Thanks."

"There is one small problem."

"About your report?"

"No. Something else, I'm afraid."

"There aren't any *small* problems, good-looking. Hit me."

"Tina and I have looked everywhere, deleted everything we could. But it appears Jon made a hard copy of the book before I reached him. He did something with it. We aren't sure what."

"Why do I hate where this is going?"

"And if I ask him, really get into his mind and ask him, it could jeopardize—"

"The footprints you've already left," I said glumly. "You think he turned it in to his prof already?"

"I . . . hope so. Because otherwise, a book-length manuscript about our lives has gone missing. And if your column catches on, someone could see it and . . ."

"Well . . . it'll probably turn up. He was doing it for school; it's not like he had some sinister motive or anything. Right? Sinclair? Right?"

"Probably." Which is as close as Mr. Buzzkill would ever get to admitting nothing would probably come of it.

"Catchy title, though," he said as we both felt the sun start to come up on Christmas Eve. *"Undead and Unwed."*

"That title sucks," I said, and then it was morning, and everything went dark, and I went wherever it is vampires go when they aren't Christmas shopping.